Maggie Boylan

Also by Michael Henson

Ransack

A Small Room with
Trouble on My Mind

Crow Call

The Tao of Longing and
the Body Geographic

The Dead Singing

Tommy Perdue

The True Story of the Resurrection
and Other Poems

MAGGIE
BOYLAN

Michael Henson

SWALLOW PRESS / OHIO UNIVERSITY PRESS

ATHENS

Swallow Press
An imprint of Ohio University Press, Athens, Ohio 45701
ohioswallow.com

First Swallow Press / Ohio University Press edition published 2018
Originally published as *The Way the World Is: The Maggie Boylan Stories*
by Brighthorse Books, 2015

Some of the stories in this collection originally appeared in *Appalachian
Heritage*, *Gray Sparrow Journal*, *Overtime*, *Pine Mountain Sand & Gravel*,
Storyscape Journal, *Superstition Review*, *Still: The Journal*,
and *Every River on Earth: Writings from Appalachian Ohio*.

To obtain permission to quote, reprint, or otherwise reproduce or
distribute material from Swallow Press / Ohio University Press
publications, please contact our rights and permissions department
at (740) 593-1154 or (740) 593-4536 (fax).

Printed in the United States of America
Swallow Press / Ohio University Press books are printed
on acid-free paper ⊗ ™

Hardcover ISBN: 978-0-8040-1201-0
Paperback ISBN: 978-0-8040-1202-7
Electronic ISBN: 978-0-8040-4091-4

28 27 26 25 24 23 22 21 20 19 18   5 4 3 2 1

Library of Congress Control Number 2017959230

The creation of this book was supported in part by
a grant from the Ohio Arts Council.

For Billy Ray Sanders

(1971–2010)

and so many others

Contents

Maggie Boylan

JAMES CARPENTER had just hung the gas pump back in its cradle and he had one foot in the door of his truck and here came Maggie Boylan, straight as a bullet, foul-mouthed, skinny, death-head-looking, Oxy-addled, thieving Maggie Boylan.

"Are you headed into town?" she called. "Can you give me a ride into town?"

He looked around him. He hated to turn down anyone in need of a ride, but still . . . this was Maggie Boylan. He thought, This could be a big mistake in the making.

Maggie was bundled into an oversized denim coat that must have belonged to her husband. It was a bright, late October day with a big wind and she staggered a moment as the wind gusted off the hills and down the highway. It tossed her hair into her eyes and she pulled a hand from the pocket of her coat to brush it back.

"I sure could use a ride," she said.

James Carpenter was, in fact, headed into town. There was no way to disguise it. He had no handy lie he could use to put her off. So he told her, "I got to drop off some papers at the courthouse and I'm coming straight back."

"That works for me," she said. "I just got to pick up some medicine for my mother-in-law."

Later, a friend would remind him: Maggie's mother-in-law had died a month before, and she had no truck with Maggie when she was alive. Later, he would see how Maggie had fooled him all along. But now, he could not see how he could turn her away.

"I got to go right now," he said. He was on a deadline and he hoped that she would have to go back to her house to get something together. Maybe she had to get her purse or maybe some papers of her own and maybe he could dodge her that way. But then, what did Maggie Boylan have left to get together?

"I'm ready," she said. "Let's roll." She pulled open the passenger-side door and launched herself into the seat even before he could get his key into the ignition. She already had her purse. It was one of these backpack purses, so he hadn't seen it earlier. She pulled it off her shoulders and began to rummage inside. "Shit," she said, then put her hand to her mouth. "Sorry, I didn't mean to cuss. You wouldn't have a lighter, would you?"

He did not.

"I should of remembered you don't smoke. Wait just a minute while I bum me a light." She planted her purse on the seat and jumped back onto the apron. "Don't worry. I won't be but half a minute."

There was a little of everything at this crossroads station just outside the little crossroads town of Wolf Creek. Off to one side, on the other side of the grocery section and the Post Office window, beyond the tools and the laundry detergent and the quarts of oil and transmission fluid, four old men sat at their coffee as they did every morning in the restaurant section in the same restaurant booth by the front window and they watched everyone who came in for a stick of beef jerky or a bag of chips or a sandwich from the deli. They were good old men, with no harm in them, retired farmers and loggers and one old part-time farmer who had been his fourth-grade teacher.

But they talked. They watched everything and they gossiped without shame. And now the story would get around that he was seen with Maggie Boylan and that story would complicate his life even more than it was already. But done is done. Maggie had him pinned there with her backpack purse on his seat, so she was on for the ride to town.

The old men did not seem to turn—it would not be right to stare—but their eyes turned to watch Maggie leave the truck and enter the store and they watched her stalk down the grocery aisle and right up to their little table where they shrugged all four of them around. Each one kept a pouch of Red Man Chew in the pocket of his coat but not a one of them smoked. Maggie had better luck with a trucker at the counter. He gave her a cigarette and a light and she came out to the truck inhaling desperately.

"You don't mind if I smoke in here, do you? I'll hold it out the window." She cranked the window down and exhaled into the open air.

"I'm so glad you could give me a ride," she said. "My mother-in-law's got that high blood pressure and you don't play with that and she can't get out on her own and she needs that medicine bad. If you hadn't come around I don't know what I would of done because these folks around here is all too proud to be seen with me, like they ain't got their own shit to deal with, pardon my French, so I really do appreciate you doing this and I don't know how I can thank you."

All this, as he cranked and cranked the ignition which, for some reason, at this moment and under the eight eyes of the four old men, had gone deader than a hammer. No horn, no dashboard light, not a whisper from the starter. So he guessed the problem. He got out, lifted the hood, and saw right away that a white crust of corrosion covered the positive post of the battery and it had chosen this under-the-eight-eyes moment, when he was already strapped for time and Maggie Boylan was perched in his cab in front of God and everybody, to break the connection. No connection, no juice. He knew the quick fix, though. He pulled a hammer from behind the seat, came back around to the battery, and gave the cable end a tap.

Just a little tap, no sense in breaking the post, but a little tap was enough to tighten the cable end onto its post, so in a moment, he had the truck started and had pulled out onto the highway toward town.

Maggie picked up the hammer and admired it. "That's an old railroad hammer, ain't it," she said.

"My grandpa worked for the B&O."

Maggie studied the hammer a moment more. "I bet it's worth some money."

He shook his head. "Flea market, couple bucks." If Maggie thought his grandfather's hammer was worth anything, it might slip away with her when she left the truck.

"You fixed that battery pretty slick," Maggie said. She set the hammer down between them on the seat. "I was afraid we'd be stuck there till tomorrow evening."

"I wish everything in life was that easy to fix."

"Don't I know it? But I always did think you was a smart one. Even when you was still a cop and you'd have to haul my drunk ass to jail and my kids'd say you was mean and all, I'd tell them, he's just doing his job, honey, and he ain't all hateful like them others."

James Carpenter remembered something entirely different. He recalled that Maggie Boylan had cursed him with names he had never been cursed before or since, names almost Biblical in their damning power, names that seemed to have been pulled full-formed from the earth, like stones or the roots of strange weeds. She had her full weight and strength back then and fought like a wet cat right out in front of those children with their eyes dark and wide.

But that was years ago and now those children were gone to foster care. Since that time, Maggie had done a stint in Marysville and a halfway house and had come back to trade the alcohol for OxyContin and the OxyContin for crack cocaine and to trade the crack back for the Oxys and whatever else she could find. And to lose half of her body weight so that now she was a spiky little burned-out sparkler of a woman, nearly weightless, withered and hollow-eyed as if she had been thrown into a kiln and dried.

"I always said it was wrong the way they done you," she said. "You was the best cop this county ever had. And I've knowed them all."

He said nothing to this. Who could stop Maggie Boylan when she was on a roll? An ambulance passed with its red lights awhirl. The wail of its siren moved up the musical scale, then down as it passed, headed toward Wolf Creek.

"That's what I want to do," Maggie said. "I want to be an EMT. They taught us CPR up in Marysville and I told myself, if I can ever get myself straight, I'm gonna go to school and get certified for that shit. I could save me some lives."

He wanted to tell her to save her own life first, but he knew she was not about to listen. He knew she would continue to talk all the way into town, which she did as he drove on, checking the condition of the fields as they passed. As she talked, they passed fields marked by shattered cornstalks and the daggers of cut tobacco and barns bulging with tobacco hung to cure, some still a pale green and others gone the color of leather. There were fields stripped black by the plow and ready for winter planting and still others unplowed, unpastured, grown over with ironweed, Johnson grass, and yarrow, surrounding farmhouses gone gray and leaning ahead of the wind.

And closer to town, there were still others, pastures or cornfields just a few years ago, now landscaped level as a putting green with long lanes leading up to houses so new and excessive that it hurt his eyes just to look at them, the new houses of people with new money or the second homes or retirement homes for people from the city.

"Anyway," Maggie said. "Everybody knows they done you wrong up there. And the ones that's left is a bunch of suck-ass perverts, God damn them all to hell." She did not apologize for cursing this time. "And after you just lost your wife from cancer. Double-damn them, that was low."

James Carpenter looked out at a gray barn hung thick with curing tobacco the color of a dull flame, and he did not hear what Maggie said next.

❖ ❖ ❖

HIS WIFE was sick for nearly a year and, for nearly a year, James Carpenter slept barely three hours a night. He went about the business of arresting drunk drivers and investigating stolen calves; he endured conferences with doctors, visits from nurses, and the indignities of home health care, all in a half-wakened, half-somnolent state, so that once the funeral was over and his daughter flew back to California, he slept for three days straight.

That made for trouble with the sheriff, but it was nothing like the trouble to come, for when he woke, he found he had developed a habit of restlessness and found himself still sleepless, alert in every cell.

At three in the insomniac morning, he walked through the rooms of his house, listening to the owls and the coyotes and thinking hard.

For the world had shifted under his feet and he was aware now of a new sense of who was wrong and who was being wronged, who was stealing and what was being stolen.

2

MAGGIE BOYLAN was a pretty girl back when she was in school. But wild. Wild enough that, at fourteen, she ran away to Nevada; at fifteen, someone had to pluck her off a railroad bridge before she jumped; at sixteen, she had her first conviction and her first child; at seventeen, eighteen, nineteen, and twenty, she had more wild times with even wilder men, a couple more children, and a rap sheet of drunk and disorderlies. There should have been a string of theft charges as well, but the only thing Maggie seemed to do well was steal, for things disappeared when she was around, things small as cigarettes and wedding rings and large as bales of hay and two-ton trucks, and she was always suspected, but never charged.

By the time James Carpenter came out of the Army and joined the county sheriff's patrol, the pretty young girl was just a memory, but the wild woman was in full force, for Maggie had the weight and muscle of a farm woman and she had the grizzle and fight of a cornered animal.

Each time Carpenter came out to the house on a call, Maggie heaped her curses on him and his partner—he knew better than to go out there alone. She fought, scratched, wrestled, and battered until they could stuff her into the backseat of a patrol car. And then, often as not, she would bang her head against the cage until her forehead bled and they would have to truss her up like an old rug and she would lay up in the cell half the night banging on the bars with a tin cup and shouting out her curses, which seemed endless in their variety and their bedrock vehemence.

Somewhere along the way, she dropped the wild men and settled on sixty acres her daddy had left her when he died. And she married a man who hoped that love would tame her. But it had not worked.

Finally, the judge sent her away for peddling amphetamines at the truck stop in Wolf Creek. She did three years in Marysville, then three months more in a halfway house, and had a tough parole officer who kept her on a short leash for another year after that. She stayed clean, Carpenter supposed, for he never had another call out to the farmhouse near the crossroads until OxyContin blew into the county like a long, ugly storm. So it started all over again.

❖　❖　❖

OXYCONTIN WAS a terrible thing. It could turn a good man into a thief, a good woman into a prostitute. It could make a farm go to seed; a house go to foreclosure.

Three days after his wife died, he caught a man in his kitchen at three in the morning. You're too late, he would have told the man if he hadn't run. Her cousin had stolen the pills from her bedside before she was even cold.

❖　❖　❖

HE ASKED her, "They still got your old man in jail?" They were near the place where the cedar woods gave way to the golf course at the edge of town.

Maggie looked at the end of her cigarette, decided there was one more draw in it, took that, and threw it out the window. "Yeah," she said. "That's another raw deal. Expired tags. That's all they got on him, expired tags. They've had him for two whole months in that little shithouse of a jail. They tried to get him for running dope and they tore his car to pieces looking and couldn't find nothing but them expired tags he was running on till his check would come in. So they took that poor man in and I don't know how I'm gonna ever make his bail and he ain't never smoked more'n a joint or two in his whole life, but they think just because I sold some drugs ten years ago, which he was never involved in, they still think they can find something on us, and the poor man ain't done nothing wrong except put up with me and raise them kids when I was in the joint."

James Carpenter had his doubts. In twenty years on the force, he had never known anyone to be held any time at all for expired tags. Rumor had doubts as well, for rumor had it that her old man took the fall for Maggie to keep her from being sent up again.

"They think because he's married to me, they can find something on him. But what they don't know is, I'm clean. Can you tell? Can you tell I've picked up weight? Seven pounds in a month. I'm off the drugs, been off for two months. Look at my eyes. See? They're clear now. They ain't got that cloud. Things ain't never going to be like they was."

James Carpenter nodded his approval. He was sure this was another one of Maggie's lies, but he had decided it was easier to go along.

My God, my God, he wondered. What have I got myself into?

❖ ❖ ❖

MAGGIE BOYLAN had once been a regular part of Carpenter's work life, but in the months since he lost his job, he had seen nothing of her at all. It was strange, and a little embarrassing, to have her now in the cab of his truck when before, she had ridden behind him in a patrol car, cuffed to the backseat and cursing.

He glanced over to her ravaged face with the bones all knocking at the doors of her flesh and tried to see in her the pretty, wild girl.

But that girl was gone, as if she had never been, chased away by smoke and needles and a flood of cheap vodka.

3

"I'LL MEET you right here," she told him in front of the drugstore. "I'll just leave this purse right here if you don't mind." She pulled out her billfold and stuffed the purse under the seat. "If I ain't on the street, I'll be in here after these prescriptions."

That was all well and good; he wanted to spend as little time in town as possible. Get in, get your business done, get out. That was how he liked it ever since the trouble with the job and all the assaults on his reputation. He had to check in with his lawyer and drop off some papers relating to his grievance and appeal. Fifteen minutes max, and he would be ready to head back home.

It took only ten minutes for James Carpenter to do what he had to do. But twenty minutes later, thirty minutes, forty minutes: Maggie Boylan was nowhere in sight. He checked briefly in the drugstore and did not see her there. He could have asked, but that would have meant telling the whole town he had been hanging out with Maggie Boylan and he did not want to feed the rumor mill. So he waited and fretted in the shadow of that damned courthouse.

He should have left her behind. Any normal person would have left her. But there was that purse under his seat. She had trapped him twice now with that purse. The wind shook the courthouse trees and skipped scrap paper across the courthouse lawn. He muttered around the block, talked to a couple of the old men on the benches of the courthouse square, went in for coffee at the Square Deal Grill, came back around, and saw her, leaning against the fender of his truck as if he was the one who was late.

She must have bummed another light. She held a cigarette close to her lips; tobacco smoke ran away from her in a gust. He was ready to tell her off for leaving him to wait so long, but she stared at the sidewalk and did not raise her eyes. Bright tears streaked her guttered cheeks.

So he held his peace. She said nothing as he got in the cab and she said nothing as she pulled herself into her seat. He asked, "Are you all right?"

"I'm all right, it's them courthouse motherfuckers. They think they rule the fucking world. Hell, they ain't even motherfuckers cause their own whorish mothers wouldn't have them."

He turned the ignition and everything was dead again.

"Oh fuck," she said. "Please get me out of this tight-ass town. I can't stand these bluenose motherfuckers with all their little sheephead smiles. Get me out of here before I kill somebody for sure."

James Carpenter looked behind the seat of the truck, but the hammer was not there. He was sure he put it back in its nest among the other tools he kept in the truck, but maybe, in his hurry at the crossroads store, he had mislaid it.

"If my old man wasn't in that jail right now, I'd blow that whole place up. I'd drop that motherfucker right around their ears, ever lying sack of shit walking those halls, just to see them buried in the rubble."

She continued to curse as he rummaged through his tools. The hammer was nowhere to be seen, so he pulled out a tire tool, which he thought a little awkward for the job. But it worked. Just a little tap, and he was able to start the truck back up.

"Yeah, I'm all right," she said. "I just want to shoot me a couple deputies." She had not stopped cursing the whole time he had tinkered with the battery and she showed no signs of stopping now. "I'd like to blow the balls off them all. If they had them, which I doubt."

Carpenter's own thoughts about the courthouse gang were not so far off from Maggie's, but he hated to stoke his resentments. "They're just doing their job, Maggie," he told her, just to remind himself.

"No they ain't. Their job ain't to keep me from visiting my own husband. Their job ain't to tell me I can't see him cause I didn't have no ID. They know damn well who I am. And if they don't, I'll sure enough let them know. They let every skank and crack whore and hustling bitch in the county visit their man, but they won't let Maggie Boylan see her man who ain't done no harm to nobody, just too damn broke to get his tags up to date."

"Maggie . . ."

"Which I'm sorry I was late, but they was ready real quick with those pills and I remembered it was visitor's day and you wasn't back yet so I thought, hell I won't be but a minute and it's right across the street and all. So I'm thinking I'll just go over there and tell Gary how I been trying to get money for his bail and all, but I got his mom to cook for and to get the pills for and I ain't had an unemployment check in over a month and I can't get nobody to explain that to me and that big old lard can that works the front desk at the jailhouse says I can't visit cause I had that little trip to Marysville."

"They got their rules."

"No they don't. They got one set of rules for themselves and another set of rules for the likes of you and me. You know they do. They didn't care about the rules when they searched my old man's car to look for dope. They didn't care about the rules when they come out to the house without a scrap of a warrant to look to see was we cooking up meth. They didn't care about the rules when they sent me off to prison with my kids crying in the gallery. And I know they didn't care about the rules when they set you up and fired you."

"Maggie, they suspended me."

"Well, we know they fired you. Don't lie."

"Maggie . . ."

"Everybody knows they set you up and they fired you. They knew you was on their case about county workers at the golf course and they knew you had their number about old Lard Bucket getting blow jobs from the girls in the jailhouse. They knew you was on their case about all the little hush-up deals that go on in the county, so they set you up."

"Maggie . . ."

"They did. Everybody knows they did."

"Maggie . . ."

"Don't lie. Everybody knows you never give that boy no fifty dollars just so you could ball that little cracked-out bitch of a girlfriend he's got. He's just a lying, snake-eyed, drug-running ex-con that'll say anything to keep from going back to Chillicothe. He'd lie on his own mother for a nickel rock. It's true. Don't lie."

"I can't say anything."

"I know. Because you got a court case and the lawyer's done told you don't talk to nobody about it. But I know. You can't bullshit a bullshitter."

"I can't say anything."

"You don't have to. I know exactly what happened. You went down to that trailer to see that little lying cunt because you thought she could tell you something about the low-life deals going down with that courthouse gang and she set you up. Didn't she?"

"I can't say."

"I could understand it if you did want to get a little off her. Old Lard Can gets his right at work. But everybody knows that's not why you was there."

"Maggie, I can't say."

"You don't need to say nothing. I know all about it."

❖ ❖ ❖

YELLOW FIELDS, black fields, gray hills in the distance. Maggie talked on. "I know what you're thinking. How does a crazy bitch like Maggie Boylan know so much about what goes on?"

Which was not exactly what he was thinking, but it was close.

"I got my ways, you see. I watch. I listen. I think for myself. I don't just take what everybody says is gospel. All them good people that look down their noses at you, all they do is think

what somebody tells them to think. Ain't a one of them thinks
for themselves. But anyway . . ."

The crossroads store was by now a half mile down the
highway, but the road to Maggie's sixty acres was just ahead on
the left. He turned on the blinkers to make ready.

"No," she said. "Just take me back to Gleason's. I got to get
me some baloney."

He hoped his grimace didn't show.

"Anyway, what I was saying, don't ever go around a little
lying whore like that without you got a witness. If you can't
get no one else, I'll go with you. Cause they'll fry your ass ever
time. You think you know these people, but you don't know
them like I do. They'll sell you out for a six pack and a carton of
cigarettes."

He pulled to the edge of the lot. His first inclination was to
let Maggie off there, on the highway shoulder, on the off chance
no one would see her climb out of his truck. But a wave of
defiance rose up in him. All his life, those old men had watched
him. And all his life, he had worried over what they thought
of him. Let them watch, he thought. They can think whatever
they want. He pulled up bold as life by the gas pumps in front
of the big restaurant window and the eight watchful eyes of
the four old men who did not disguise their staring this time as
Maggie stepped bold as life out of the truck.

Maggie stood a moment in the open door with her old man's
coat pulled up around her ears. The wind skipped a plastic bottle
across the pavement and she shivered the coat higher on her
shoulders. "They'll leave you to hang," she said. "And won't a
soul stand behind you when they do."

She reached under the seat for her purse and pulled something
else out with it. "Here's your hammer you was missing." She smiled,
sweet and sly. She laid the prodigal hammer on the seat and started
to pull her purse onto her shoulders.

Later, back home, after the wind died down, he would go out
to clean up his battery's corroded posts and to put the hammer
back in its place. He would find, on the floor of the passenger

side, the empty bag from the pharmacy. Stapled to the bag, he would see the slip of paper that told what was in it. It would be none of his business to look, but he would look anyway and he would see nothing for high blood pressure and he would know then that Maggie Boylan had gotten stoned on her dead mother-in-law's Oxys right there in his truck and he, Maggie's fool, had not noticed a thing.

But at that moment, as she stood in the open door, with the big wind pulling at the wings of her coat, he felt ready to tell Maggie Boylan he would wait. He was ready to give her a ride to the house. He was ready to defy the stares and the talk. He was ready to make the big mistake.

Instead, he told her, "You take care, Maggie."

"If you ever need me for anything," she said, "you know where I am." Then she turned and walked away. The wind gusted across the lot and blew up a great column of dust and paper scrap. Maggie staggered a moment in the wind and turned to say something more. But the wind tore the words away. She staggered again and maybe it was the wind or maybe it was the Oxys. James Carpenter knew that Maggie Boylan, Oxy-addled, thieving Maggie Boylan, was wasted down to the near side of nothing. But in her oversized coat she looked slim as a girl.

Black Friday

IT WAS the day after Thanksgiving at the Once Removed secondhand store and Maggie Boylan burst through the door, already talking. Sarah Hunter was on the phone with her mother, her poor sick mother in Columbus, but you could not shush Maggie Boylan.

"Sarah, I got to get some money," Maggie said. She was dressed in a big, loose, oversized denim coat with the sleeves rolled back, jeans all out at the knees, and a pair of men's work boots. But she held out a pair of shoes—flawlessly white walkers like nurses wear and a pair of jeans, crisp and new and embroidered with flowers and spangles, hung over the shoulder of that big loose coat.

Sarah Hunter had hoped for more customers today. She had put up her Christmas decorations and she had discounted some of the better items. But there had been hardly anybody in all day. Now, at midafternoon, two women stood over by the children's bin, rummaging for school clothes. They eyed Maggie carefully. They were in their own big coats. They continued to turn over jumpers and T-shirts but their eyes worked back and forth from Maggie to Sarah to the bin.

Maggie set the shoes and the jeans on the counter where Sarah could not miss them.

"Hold on," Sarah said into the phone. "I'm getting interrupted."

"I need you to help me," Maggie said, "Christmas is coming up. I got to get my babies' presents out of layaway."

"Let me call you back," Sarah told her mother. "I got to deal with something here."

"You know I'm sober now," Maggie said. "Can you tell? I'm getting fat."

Maggie was not getting fat. She raised her shirt to show her belly and she was not fat at all. Her ribs were like a line of coat hangers; her belly was gaunt. In fact, Maggie Boylan was all elbows and knees; she flopped about in her open coat like a horsefly inside a tent. Sarah Hunter had known Maggie since they both were girls. They had grown up friends and she could not bear to look at the hollow of her belly. She could not bear to look at the bones of her face.

"See? No more of that crack. No more Oxys. I can't live without my Vicodin on account of my back, but I don't do no more of that crack."

Sarah looked at the shoes and the jeans. Brand new; neither had ever been worn. But there was no tag on either one. "Where'd you get these, Maggie?"

"I got them for myself," Maggie said. "But my babies come first. How about ten dollars for each. Those are fifty-dollar jeans."

"Maggie, where'd you get them?"

"I got them at Target."

Sarah shot her a skeptical eye.

"I swear," Maggie said. "I wouldn't lie to you."

Dennis Hunter limped out from the back office with a stomp and a shuffle. He was in his coveralls and he had a wrench in his hand. The truck was up on ramps out back and muffler parts were strewn across the yard. He had been stomping and shuffling in and out for tools and warmth all day.

"There's your old man," Maggie said. "He's the one I want to talk to." She grabbed up the shoes and the jeans. "Hey, Dennis," she called. "Dennis," she said. "I got to talk to you." She pushed him back into the office and slammed shut the door.

"Well damn," said one of the women at the children's bin. The women looked at one another, raised brows, looked down for a moment, then back to the office door. The first woman asked, "You gonna leave her alone with your man like that?"

"If it was me," the second one said. "I'd bust that up real quick."

Sarah Hunter would have joked about it if she had been in a joking mood. But she did not trust these two and her mother was sick and she was in no mood.

"You got to watch Maggie Boylan like a hawk," the first woman said.

"I won't let her in my house no more."

"The jeans, she might have got legal, but those shoes is definitely hot."

"They probably come straight out of Walmart."

"Or Payless."

"Or Pay-Nothing."

"She comes in your house, you got to watch her ever minute. If she ain't stealing now, it's cause she's casing the joint for later."

"Ever time she comes in my house I end up with something missing."

"Like your CD player."

"She got that for sure. I can't prove it . . ."

"But you know."

"That's why I don't let her in my house no more."

"And hell if she ain't doing crack. She had to stand up twice to make a shadow."

"She must of lost fifty pounds."

Sarah interrupted. "Well," she said, then trailed off. She did not know what to say, exactly, but she wanted to hear what was going on in that office.

"You sure you want to leave Maggie back there with your old man?"

Sarah tapped a cigarette out of her pack. She could hear Maggie Boylan from behind the door. Her husband's quieter, gravel-yard voice was in there too, but not so often as Maggie's. Sarah tapped her cigarette on the counter.

"She kind of give you the brush-off, didn't she?"

"She knows I won't put up with none of her bull."

"And she thinks he will?"

Sarah shrugged. "I reckon he can handle Maggie Boylan."
She was not at all sure he could handle Maggie Boylan, but
she was not about to tell these two. She was of half a mind to
go to the office and bust them up, but she lit her cigarette, put
her elbows on the counter, and waited. She kept an eye on the
women at the children's bin, too. They might talk about Maggie,
but the two of them were not above slipping a little something
into the oversize pockets of their coats—a little dress if they
liked it, or a pair of shoes. They would be happy to have Sarah
turn her back.

The first woman held up a child-size blouse with a frilled
collar. "What do you want for this one?"

"What's it say?"

"It don't have a tag."

"Look again."

"It don't have a tag."

"Two dollars."

The woman raised a brow.

"Buck-fifty, then."

The women shuffled and bargained over a few more items
before Maggie banged open the back-office door.

"Thank you," she said. "Thank you so much."

She continued to thank her way up the aisle. "Thank you,"
she said again. "You don't know what this means. My babies can
have a merry Christmas."

"Bless you both," she said to Sarah, then banged her way out
the door and into the street.

Dennis limped behind her with the shoes and the jeans.
"You reckon these'll sell?"

Sarah Hunter tried to keep it to a whisper, but it was hard
to do. "If you want to sell them," she said, "get yourself a store
and sell them yourself. Personally, I don't want nothing to do
with them."

"Why not?"

"Cause they're hotter than a two-dollar pistol."

"She said she bought them herself."

"And didn't show no receipt to prove it. And the tags is off but they never been worn. And here's Maggie Boylan, the biggest thief in five counties telling you some bonehead story. And you think they ain't stolen."

The two women at the children's bin decided it was time to settle up. Sarah rang them up and bagged them up and helped them out the door, all with one critical eye on her husband.

She waited until the women had started gossiping down the street before she lit into him for real.

"What," she wanted to know, "did you think you were doing?"

"I bought some clothes. We're in the business of selling clothes."

"Think a minute."

"Think what?"

"Where's Maggie Boylan gonna get the money for clothes like that?"

"How do I know?"

"Her old man's been in jail all these months because he took the hit for her and all's she can do for him is to sit out in that little house in the country and stay high on OxyContin. She ain't got one dime to rub against another and she's gonna come in here with some new kicks and a pair of britches look like they come off of Shania Twain's ass and it don't occur to you there might be something fishy about the whole damn deal?"

He shrugged. He was good for errands and for fixing things up, but he had no business sense at all.

He started back to the office.

"So how much did you give her?"

"Twenty bucks."

"Twenty bucks!"

"Twenty bucks."

"You know she's probably smoked your twenty bucks by now. Or she's put it up her nose. You know it ain't for no Christmas toys in layaway."

He rattled around in the back room looking for his tool. "Do you know where that hacksaw went?"

"Do I ever use a hacksaw?"

"I thought I'd ask."

"So what were you two talking about for so long back there?"

"About how her kids wouldn't have no Christmas if she couldn't put some money down on layaway. How they got her old man locked up over nothing. How the county's keeping her from seeing her kids . . ."

"Because she's an unfit mother."

"So I felt sorry for her."

"I reckon you felt a little more than that."

"What are you saying?"

"You know what I mean."

"Now you're talking crazy."

"You were thinking with the wrong head. That's what I was saying."

He waved the hacksaw at her and clumped and shuffled out the back door.

❖   ❖   ❖

TWENTY MINUTES later, a girl stalked in with metal in her lip and a shaky fire in her eye. She looked straight at Sarah and asked, "Has Maggie Boylan been in here?" Her fire died quickly and she lost the track of Sarah's eye. Then she became just a girl with metal studs in her lips and nose, a nervous young girl who could not look Sarah in the eye. And that was what gave Sarah the clue.

"She stole my clothes and I want to know has she been in here?"

Sarah shot Dennis another glance—this time it was an I-told-you-so glance.

"I know she's going around trying to sell my stuff, so I want to know has she been in here?" She pulled a bulky, spangled purse off her shoulder and set it on the counter.

Sarah pulled the shoes and the jeans from behind the counter. "These look familiar?"

"They're familiar enough. How much did she get you for?"

Sarah silenced her husband with another sharp glance. "She didn't get us too bad," she said.

"I don't have anything to pay you with."

"Then don't pay nothing."

"Well, I hate for you to have to take the hit for what she done." She sucked in her lower lip and chewed on a stud. She reached for the shoes, but Sarah set her hands across them.

"She'll get hers in the end," Sarah said.

"I reckon."

"She'll do the wrong person and that'll be the end of Maggie Boylan."

"Yes, ma'am."

Sarah folded the shoes and the jeans together and put them in the spangled bag. "If she ain't died of an overdose first," she said.

"She sure could," the girl said. She stretched out her hand for the bag, but Sarah held on a moment more. "It's a shame," Sarah said. "I knew her when she was a girl and she was as good a girl growing up as there was."

The girl nodded, but she did not seem to hear. She was eager to get out the door. She put the bag under her arm, nodded briefly, and turned toward the street.

Sarah followed her out the door, then watched from the front step. The girl ran to the corner, got into a car, started it up, and pulled into the street.

And sure enough, there in the shotgun seat, sat Maggie Boylan, smoking a cigarette, and laughing. Laughing like this was the biggest joke in the world.

The bitch.

❖   ❖   ❖

FOR THE rest of the afternoon, her man continued to work on the truck. They would need the truck for pickup and delivery and that was the sort of thing Dennis was good for. It was cold to be working out of doors and it was hard work with all the heavy parts and climbing up under the truck, and his mangled leg hurt him. So every half hour or so he stumped and shuffled in for coffee and to warm his hands. She said nothing more about Maggie Boylan and the girl with metal in her mouth. She had said enough. He said nothing at all.

She tried to call her mother back and got no answer. She straightened the children's bin and handled customers and totaled up the day's receipts. Finally, near closing time, as the short day darkened, she heard the truck fire up. It hummed with a nice new-muffler hum. She heard his step, stomp and shuffle, stomp and shuffle, into the back office and the clink and clank as he put his tools away.

"Are you done back there?" He did not answer. He stomped and shuffled and clanked as if he had decided to move everything in the room.

"Say," she said again, "you about done in there?"

She heard him stomp and she heard him shuffle and heard him clink and clank.

He'll be a minute, she thought. She turned the store lights out and went to the window to flip over the CLOSED sign. A line of Christmas lights ran around the window. She could see other lights up and down the street and she could see the lights of the crèche on the courthouse square and she decided to leave her lights on like the rest.

She took out another cigarette and lit it. He would stretch out his shuffling and clanging as long as he could just so as not to talk to her. He would get over it soon enough, but he might not talk the whole way home.

I reckon she could have done it to get her old man some cigarette money, she thought. She would like that to be true. She knew it was unlikely, but she wished something like that could be true.

But no, she thought. Maggie's bought herself something to smoke or snort. And when that's gone she will pass off those shoes and those jeans on some new sucker. And then that girl will come right after with her little lie, and then they'll go on to the next.

Her man stomped and shuffled in the back office and Sarah Hunter stood in the window and smoked her cigarette. Christmas lights dressed every window up and down the square and around the courthouse and even over the door of the jail where Maggie's husband sat out his sentence. The bud of a cough had set up in the back of her throat, the bud of a tear in her eye. I should quit these things, she thought. She wished she had quit them long ago. She wished things were different in so many ways. She wished she were able to take care of her mother. She wished Maggie had not become such a wreck of a woman. She heard her man clanging and shuffling in the back and she wished she had not learned to sharpen her tongue.

She wished she could take back this whole damn story.

The Way the World Is

"THAT'S THE way the world is," the girl said. And she did not seem to like it.

"Honey, you ain't seen nothing," Maggie Boylan wanted to say. But the girl did not skip a beat.

"All I did was take her in because she was homeless and I get throwed in jail for what she done."

A late November wind rattled the windows of the lobby where they sat, side-by-side on a bench. The girl was a heavy girl—a young woman, really, but to Maggie Boylan, just a girl. She was thick in the body, weighted in the shoulders, heavy in the cheeks and around her eyes. She was pierced in several places, pierced in one nostril, pierced with a ring in her brow, pierced by an arc of studs in her ear.

"There I was," she said, "coming out the door at Walmart. I had a cart full of groceries and diapers and what not. I was fixing to feed her and her kids right along with mine, and all of a sudden, you'd of thought I was Osama Bin Laden. There goes the alarm ringing and here come the security cop and a few minutes later here come the police and there's my little kids crying and these cops want to know did I think I was smart trying to get away without paying for that purse and I'm, like, what purse?

"And what it was, that penniless bitch I took in off the street had snuck this purse she wanted into my cart after I done checked out so she skips on ahead. She borrowed my car keys, you see, and she says, I'll go ahead and unlock the door. And she skips out like there ain't nothing going on."

"She set you up."

"She didn't have the guts to steal it herself and she figured if anybody was gonna get caught it'd be me. And she would of got away with it, except I pointed her out and they ended up taking both of us to jail. And I'm thinking, there's my little kids off to foster care, and they're crying their little hearts out. And my parents had to come up from Wilsonville to fetch my kids and bail me out."

Maggie Boylan had been nodding as the girl spoke, but she perked up her ears at the mention of the children almost gone to foster care. She was small as the girl was large, small-boned and spare of flesh with the quick, fierce eyes and sharp features of a fox. She watched the girl more closely now.

"But that's the way the world is," the girl said again. "You try to help somebody and you get stiffed."

A deputy passed through the lobby. He was a heavy man with a heavy tread and he called out, "What d'you know, Maggie?"

"I know I want to visit my old man," she called. But the deputy slung himself through the door without another word.

The girl had lit a cigarette; she blew out smoke and nodded. "That's just how they treat you," she said.

"They won't let you smoke in the building." Maggie pointed to a sign above the counter.

The girl raised a skeptical brow. "They can't do no more to me than what they done already." But she drew on her cigarette one more time, stubbed it out carefully on the rim of a trashcan, then slid it back into the pack.

"They can slap you with a fine," Maggie said. "They can write you a ticket in a heartbeat."

"Right now, I don't hardly care. They could throw me right back in that cell and I wouldn't care."

"Honey, you don't know what you're saying."

"They couldn't do me no worse than what they done already. What could they do worse than what they already done?"

Maggie held her peace.

"This is the worst that's ever happened to me," the girl said. She folded her arms, unfolded them, then placed her hands on her knees "I ain't never been inside a jail before. Never did expect to be. But there I was. And all because I wanted to help some girl that wouldn't help herself."

She looked toward the door where the deputy had gone and folded her arms again.

"Like I say," she continued. "If it hadn't been for my parents coming up to make my bail, I probably would of lost my kids to foster care. And God only knows what would of happened to them."

"How many you got?"

"I got a boy and I got a girl. Three and two."

"Little tiny ones."

The girl's shoulders sagged as if she carried a world of care. "That's why I couldn't stand to see her homeless and all. Cause she got three, and all of them under six. Ain't even in school yet. So I understand what it is to have kids and you want them safe and fed and all. She comes to me complaining how she's homeless and their daddy beat on her and she had to take them kids of hers and leave home. Well, big-hearted me, I had to take them in off the street.

"So I asked her, why in the world would you do something like this to somebody trying to help you out? She says, well I reckoned you're smart and you know how to talk to people and if you got caught you'd talk your way out of it because you didn't know it was there. And I told her, 'Well, it didn't work out like that, did it?'"

Maggie had been staring at the door, but now she turned to the girl. "You want to smoke that cigarette?"

"Ma'am?"

"You still want to smoke? Let's go outside."

"I can't. I'm waiting for that bitch that put me in here."

"Come on, you can whup her ass later."

"I ain't planning to whip her ass." She stood, with a glance toward the counter. "But I do plan to give her a piece of my mind."

"You better." Maggie led the girl out onto the front steps of the courthouse. Out in the yard, a trusty pushed a pile of leaves against the wind. "You sure don't want to whup some girl's ass in the courthouse; they'll slap you in a cell inside a cell. They'll stroke you good. If you want to whip her ass, you got to go somewhere else."

"No," the girl said. She pulled out her pack and tapped out the cigarette she had stubbed out before. "I ain't a violent person. I just want her to know what I got to say."

The steps of the courthouse were cold. They cupped hands for a windbreak, lit their cigarettes, and smoked and shivered together.

"I mean," the girl said, "it just don't make sense. You pick somebody up out of the gutter and you feed their children like they was your own. You do everything it says in the Bible to do. And here I get arrested for the very first time in my life. And I don't do drugs. I don't drink. I don't do nothing. I just go to work and clean house and take care of my kids and now I probably got this on my record."

"You done?" Maggie nodded toward the cigarette.

The girl was not. Maggie had hit hers hard; she had barely stopped to breathe. She flicked the butt of it ten feet out into the yard. "Let's get out of this wind," she said.

For a second time, the girl stubbed out her cigarette. This time, she dropped it into the shrubs.

The heavy deputy was at the counter when they came back in. He glanced up from some paperwork and nodded. "You staying clean, Maggie?"

"When can I see him, Burke?"

"Tuesday. Visiting day."

"But I can't come on Tuesday."

"Can't help you, Maggie." He turned and took his papers into an inner office.

"He's the nice one," the girl said. "That other one—I ain't seen him yet today—he was mean."

"What was his name?"

"I don't know. I don't know any cops' names. Never did need to know any cops' names."

"Ain't none of them nice far as I'm concerned. Especially that one."

"At least he didn't say nothing smart, like that other one."

There was a stir in the inner office and both looked up.

"That's her," the girl said. "That's the bitch that got me arrested."

"That scrawny thing? Hell, you could whup her ass with one hand." The scrawny thing wore an oversize coat and kept losing her arms in the sleeves. She had long hair strung back behind her ears that fell down every few seconds into her eyes, so that she was in constant motion to pull back her sleeve, tuck back her hair, shift her feet, pick up a pen, sign where the deputy pointed, set down the pen, adjust her hair, and lose her arms again in her sleeves.

"Nervous little bitch, ain't she?"

"What're they doing?"

"Looks like they're fixing to let her go."

"About time. I posted her bond an hour ago."

"You done what?"

The girl shrugged.

"After everything that shifty little bitch done you?"

"Who else is gonna do it? She don't have nobody else."

"Well I'll be damned." Maggie stood, went to the counter, and called, "Burke, Tom Burke, when can I visit my old man?"

"Tuesday, Maggie. Visiting day is Tuesday."

"But I ain't got no ride for Tuesday. I got a ride today."

"There's nothing I can do about it, Maggie."

"At least let me leave him some money while I got it."

"Tuesday."

"I got twenty dollars to give him for cigarettes."

"He'll live."

"At least let me get him a can of Bugler and some papers."

The deputy shut the door.

"Fucking prick!" Maggie shouted. "Fat fuck probably shut the door so he could collect his blow job. Possum-headed punk ain't never worked the starch out of that uniform, but he can tell me Tuesday when I know damn well what day visiting day is. All he can say to me is, 'What d'you know, Maggie?' I'll tell you what I know. I know he was my old man's buddy growing up but he's too good to do me a turn even for his buddy's sake. And then he wants to know am I staying clean, as if that's any business of his."

She turned to the girl on the bench. "You want to talk about the way the world is. Well, that right there's the way the world is. Your old man is doing six months in this little rat hole jail over some bullshit and you can't even get to see him because some shit in a uniform can't do you a little favor."

"I know what you mean," the girl said.

"No, you don't know what I mean. Not till you done what I done. Not till you seen what I seen. Not till you heard them bars slam shut behind you and you know it'll be two long years before you get to hold your babies again. Then you come and tell me what the world is like."

"You're pushing your luck, Maggie," the deputy called from behind the door.

"I ain't had no luck since the day I was born."

❖ ❖ ❖

MAGGIE'S RIDE back home was still at the pool hall and might be there another hour yet, or even two.

"Yes," the neighbor boy told her. "I'm going to town, but just long enough to cash my check." Then, "Half an hour," he told her when she found him at the pool hall.

Then, "Just let me finish this rack" when she came back around.

So now she stood out on the courthouse steps, shivering in her jeans jacket, cursing softly.

She had a cigarette in one hand and her twenty-dollar bill balled up in the other and she smoked and shivered until she had smoked the cigarette down to a nub. The jailhouse door swung open and out came the scrawny thing and the heavy girl right behind her.

"What do you want me to do?" the scrawny thing said. "I already told you I'm sorry."

"You can tell my mom and dad why they had to drive all the way up here and bail me out."

A gust of wind snatched away the rest of their words and Maggie watched them take their argument up the street and around the corner.

That's the way the world is, Maggie thought. One damn fuss after another.

She looked across to the pool hall. Half an hour, she thought. It's been that long at least. That boy's liable to be there till closing time. What do I do till then?

The wind picked up a scatter of leaves and blew them across the yard and in the rattle of the leaves it seemed she could hear the scrawny thing and the heavy girl going at it hammer and tongs.

Not another soul was out. She reckoned there were people drinking coffee at the Square Deal Grill and people in line at the bank and one or two that stood at the drugstore counter for a prescription. But the wind had driven everyone off the streets and off the square. The trusty's rake leaned against a wall.

Leaves had gathered under the shrubs, leaves in the gutters, leaves on the windshields of the parked cars.

She looked at her sweaty, balled-up twenty and wished she would not do what she was likely now to do. She crossed the street and looked into the window of the pool hall. The neighbor boy stared at the table and slowly chalked his cue. Another broke a new rack.

So she had time, plenty of time by the look of it. That neighbor boy would play out every dollar in his pocket before he drove her back to Wolf Creek. And then he would want to dun her for gas money, and all she had in life was that twenty.

Her hands began to tremble; she began to ache in every bone at the thought of all that dead time and the money getting hot in her hand. She knew where she could get something for her twenty, something that would ease her mind and take away

the ache and blunt the hard edges of memory and the world,
something that would set the world aright.

The next gust of wind pushed hard against her. The snows
of December were just around the corner. She shivered at the
thought and gripped her twenty hard. It was ten cold miles
back to Wolf Creek. She looked toward the jailhouse where
her old man sat in his cell, then through the pool hall window
where the boys were racking up another game. She hesitated
for another moment, then with a curse for the neighbor boy, for
Deputy Burke, for the heavy young girl and the scrawny thing,
she followed her twenty down the alley.

Timothy Weatherstone

IT WAS Timothy Weatherstone's first day as a deputy and his first official act was to take the cuffs off Maggie Boylan. Insufficient evidence, said her lawyer. Case dismissed, said the judge.

"Score one for you, Maggie," said the sheriff.

"I didn't know we was keeping score."

"Oh, we're keeping score," he said. "And one of these days, we'll win." The sheriff was lean as a fox, dressed in his sharp-pressed, black-and-gray uniform with gold sunrise patches at the shoulders and a shining gold badge on his chest. Maggie was lean as well, but perilously lean, like a fox half-starved. She wore a sweatshirt and blue jeans busted out at the bony knees. "So you're free to go," the sheriff said. "Until next time."

She looked at the sheriff and then looked away as if she might spit but thought the better of it. She rubbed her wrists where the cuffs had bit them, then looked up to see who had set her loose. "Timmy Weatherstone, is that you?"

Weatherstone winced to hear Maggie call him "Timmy." He was sure that Tom Burke, the other deputy in the room, was grinning behind his back. Here he was, the rookie, fresh out of college, trying to prove himself, trying to stand up as a professional, and first thing, he gets called "Timmy" by the likes of Maggie Boylan, raggedy, strung-out, withered-to-the-bone Maggie Boylan.

"You don't remember me," she said. "But I used to hang with your mother when you was just a baby."

He did not remember, but he knew the stories and did not want to be reminded.

"We used to call her Aunt Jenny, she was so good to us spite of all her trouble. I used to give you your bottle and change your diaper. That was before she got saved and quit running with us wild young girls. And now you're a deputy."

"It's his first day on the job, Maggie," said the sheriff. "Don't ruin it for him."

"I wouldn't ruin nothing for him," Maggie said. "He worked too hard to get here." She stood to put on her coat—a big, blue denim barn coat that hung off her shoulders and covered her hands so that she had to roll back the cuffs. "He could of been on this side of the table, except he straightened up."

"That was years ago, Maggie," said the sheriff.

"You're right. He's made something of himself," she said. "If your mother was here, she'd be proud."

Tim Weatherstone did not want to hear his mother mentioned by the likes of Maggie Boylan and would have said so. But after six months, even at the mention of his mother, the words still piled up in his throat.

The sheriff pointed to Maggie's tent of a coat. "Isn't that Gary's jacket?"

"I don't reckon it's none of your business, but yes it's his jacket. He don't need it where you got him."

"No, I don't suppose he does."

She looked into the property bin. "Is this everything?"

"You signed the receipt."

"But I had a ten-dollar bill in my pocket."

"You signed the receipt, Maggie. It says fifty-seven cents on the receipt. Fifty-seven cents is what you get."

Maggie glared at Thomas Burke and he looked away.

"You were intoxicated at the time you signed that receipt," the sheriff said. "You might have been in a blackout." He looked at Maggie and he looked at the deputy with the sharp edge of his eye.

"Somebody blacked me out of my money," Maggie said. She muttered something else, low and indecipherable, and continued to mutter as she signed for the rest of her property.

"What would you do with ten dollars anyway, Maggie?"

"I'd walk over to the Square Deal Grill and get me something to eat for one thing, cause what you people feed a body ain't fit to patch a sidewalk."

"Gary seems to like it good enough."

"Gary don't speak up for hisself like I do."

"No, I don't suppose he does," the sheriff said. "But then, you can't please everybody."

"Well, it'll please me to get the fuck out of here." She pushed back the sleeves of her coat and picked up her fifty-seven cents. She stuffed the coins into the pocket of her jeans, looked up at Tim Weatherstone, and gave him a once-over from the badge on his chest to his spit-polished shoes.

"I don't reckon you could give me a ride home, could you, Timmy?"

"You got a free ride here, Maggie," the sheriff said. "You only get the one."

"I didn't ask you," she said.

"But he answers to me."

Maggie gave Tim Weatherstone the once-over once again and said, "You look good, Timmy, all spiffed out and trim and ironed all sharp. You done good for yourself. Just don't forget . . ."

She paused and rubbed her wrists again. She glanced a reproach toward Burke and one toward the sheriff, then looked back to Timothy Weatherstone and said, "Don't forget where you come from."

❖ ❖ ❖

TIMOTHY WEATHERSTONE knew where he came from. He came from a house a mile up the holler road from Maggie Boylan herself, though the house he lived in was now, six months after his mother's death, nearly bare as the cell of a monk. His older brother and his older sister had come down, one from Cleveland, the other from Columbus, each with a pickup truck and a list. They left him with a bed, a dresser, a kitchen table, four rooms full of echoes, and some pictures on the walls.

❖ ❖ ❖

AS SOON as Maggie Boylan was out the door, the sheriff was on his feet. He checked to be sure she was gone down the hall, then he went to the window to be sure she was gone out of the building. Satisfied, he called Deputy Burke into his office.

Tom Burke rose. He was a big man, round at the gut and round at the shoulders, and he rose slowly. Weatherstone, who had the lean body of a runner, watched him with a mixture of pity and contempt. It must take two full yards of leather, he thought, just to make his gun belt.

"Sit down," the sheriff said. Then he kicked shut the door.

Weatherstone could hear only that the sheriff spoke loud and the deputy soft and the sheriff spoke long and the deputy short, and if he could have figured out anyplace else to go, Weatherstone would have gone there, for he did not want to see the deputy in his shame as he did when, finally, Burke emerged with his face red and his jaw clenched.

Without a word, Burke stepped to the desk, pulled a set of keys out of a drawer and slammed it shut. "You ever serve an eviction before?" Before Weatherstone could answer, he said, "That's what I thought. Come on, I got to show you how it's done."

He handed Weatherstone a clipboard with a Notice to Vacate attached and walked out the door without waiting to see if Weatherstone followed. In spite of his weight, he was down the stairs and through the lobby, across the parking lot and into the driver's seat of the cruiser before Weatherstone could catch up and get his hand on the passenger door. He was barely in his seat and not yet buckled in when the deputy threw the cruiser into gear and punched it. The tires barked and kicked up gravel as he pulled out of the lot and into the street and they chittered all the way down Court Street and around the corner at Main.

Weatherstone glanced at the Notice. He did not know the name, but he knew the place and he knew it was near a gravel quarry on the western edge of the county. But they were headed east and Weatherstone wondered, but he thought it better not to ask.

In moments, they were on the eastern edge of town where the golf course bordered the cedar woods that ran unbroken to the farms along Wolf Creek. A hundred yards past the city line, there was Maggie Boylan, backward-walking down the gravel shoulder.

She saw the cruiser and she turned and began to walk forward.

"Now look at that," Burke said. "She's flipped us the bird." He laughed. "She's making good time," he said. "But she's got a long walk if she walks it all. Nine miles out and then a couple miles up the holler."

Weatherstone knew exactly how far Maggie had to walk. He ran past her house nearly every night. Right across the road from Maggie, a dealer's house perched at the top of what they called Pillhead Hill, so she once she got home, she needn't go far to get what she wanted.

Burke slowed the car to match her pace. He told Weatherstone to roll down his window and he leaned forward to speak past him. "You wouldn't be hitchhiking, would you, Maggie?"

"No, I wouldn't. That would be illegal."

"You certainly appeared to be hitchhiking."

"I certainly appeared to be looking back to see who was likely to run me over."

"You wouldn't lie to me, would you Maggie?"

"Never in my life."

"Then why did you lie about me back at the office?"

"That ten dollars? That wasn't a lie. And you know it wasn't a lie."

"Do you just like the thought of making me look bad?"

"I don't need to make you look bad. You do that all on your own." She stopped and faced him so that he had to brake the cruiser. "I might lie to get myself out of trouble," she said. "But I never lie somebody into trouble. You took my ten dollars and you bought you a blow job from some girl who couldn't make bail and you did it just because you could."

"Now you just lied again, and in front of this impressionable young man."

"It ain't no lie, motherfucker."

"What did you just call me?"

"I'll tell you what I called you. I called you a liar and a thief." She leaned toward the window to look past Tim Weatherstone. "Liar," she said. "Thief."

The deputy tapped Weatherstone at the elbow. "You heard her," he said. "You're a witness."

"Don't pull him into your bullshit," Maggie said.

"Just stay right where you are," said Burke. "I think I need to write you a ticket."

"Ticket for what? Minding my own business?"

"Disorderly conduct," the deputy said. "You cuss out a deputy, that's disorderly."

"Disorderly? You want to see disorderly? I can show you disorderly." She kicked the cruiser door, turned, and began to walk away. "Fuck you," she called. "I'm taking my disorderly self home."

The deputy pulled the cruiser onto the shoulder. "Fleeing and eluding," he called. "Obstruction of justice. Resisting arrest."

Maggie launched a string of curses into the wind.

"I believe I heard a threat. That would be a charge of menacing."

Maggie's curses flew out of her like a flock of crows.

"Come on back, Maggie. I got to give you these tickets."

She continued to unfurl curses into the wind and Tom Burke laughed. He put the cruiser back into gear, hit the light bar, scratched off the gravel of the shoulder, pitched the cruiser into a sharp U-turn, and headed west.

❖ ❖ ❖

THEY DELIVERED the eviction notice to an old man in a little, wind-battered trailer set on a weedy patch of ground above the river. The quarry had chewed up the acres to within a hundred yards of where the trailer sat. They could hear the roar and clank of the dozers and the trucks at work. Gray columns of dust rose from the pit and dispersed among the blackened ironweed and yellowed foxtail of the overgrown pasture that was left.

At the trailer, a splitting maul leaned against a chopping block near the porch and firewood was stacked neat as pie inside a converted corncrib. Wood smoke puffed comfortably from the chimney of the trailer.

In spite of the nip of a December wind, the old man sat out on the front step of his trailer, as if he had been expecting them. He rose from his step when they pulled into the yard and stood with his hands in his pockets, straight and slim as a hoe handle but not nearly so smooth.

"What's with all the water jugs?" the deputy asked. They were lined up on either side of the steps, full jugs to the left, empties to the right.

"The quarry sunk my well. I got to haul water from here and there, wherever I can get it."

"Well, the quarry wants you off the property anyway." The deputy showed the old man the eviction notice on the clipboard.

The old man glanced down at the clipboard, but he did not move to pick it up.

"If you sign, it just means you received it. It doesn't mean you agree with it."

"It's my property."

"That's not what the quarry says."

The old man spat a slim brown spear of tobacco juice off to the side. "The quarry don't own it," he said. "I own it."

The deputy shrugged. "I reckon that's for the court to decide. Do you want me to read this to you?"

"I can read."

"Well then, do you want to sign?"

The old man sat down. He spat again, then looked up at Timothy Weatherstone. "Ain't you Jenny Weatherstone's boy?"

Weatherstone nodded. Burke said, "It's his first day on the job. Let's don't make this difficult." He reached out with the clipboard again. The old man looked down at it but did not move.

"I'm gonna write down 'Refused to Sign' and I'm gonna leave your copy right here." He pulled the Notice from out of the clipboard and set it on the chopping block. He picked up a chunk of wood and set it on top of the paper so it wouldn't blow away. "You can do what you want with it, but if you want to appeal, you have ten days to do it. Ten days. If you get you a lawyer and take your case to court you might not win, but you're likely to get a better deal. If not, they'll send us back out here on day eleven and we'll have to pull you off the property."

The old man spat, imperfectly, at nothing in particular, and in no particular direction.

❖ ❖ ❖

HALFWAY BACK to town, the deputy looked over to Timothy Weatherstone and asked, "What do you reckon is going to happen? Do you think that old man is gonna appeal?"

If Burke wanted an answer, he didn't wait to hear it. "He won't," he said. "He's too damn mean and he's too damn stubborn and if he wasn't, he's still too damn poor to get a lawyer and who knows if there's even a lawyer in this county that'd take on such a tangle as this. So we'll be back out here shortly to set him out. He's got nowhere to go, but we're gonna set him out anyway. Meanwhile, this whole county is going to hell. You know that, don't you? Between the drugstores and the druggies and the doctors and the dealers, I can't tell which is worst. You get a dozen ODs on a Saturday night in one little country hospital. And what are we doing about it? Not a goddam thing. We got time to chase some old man off his property, which somebody stole out from under his nose. We got time to ticket some half-starved logger for running his truck without tags and

we got time to take some strung-out chick's kids to foster care—
which, by the way, is what we did to Maggie Boylan two years
ago—but we can't stop the fucking Oxy and the Percocets and
the Vicodins and it don't even look like we're trying. And it
won't be about five minutes before the heroin starts rolling in.

"Just look at the jailhouse, there's what, eight, ten people in
there. I bet you dollars to donuts ever last one of them has got
Oxy in his story. And by the way, I did take Maggie's ten dollars,
in case you're wanting to know."

Weatherstone did not really want to know, but he nodded
and said nothing.

"I know what you're thinking. My little run-in with Maggie
Boylan out on the highway was over the top. Which it was. But
do you know why I took her ten dollars? Maggie always says
she's gonna bring her old man some money, but she never does.
So I did it for her. I took it and I gave it to Gary so he could
buy him a pack of Bugler. Maggie will tell you what great things
she's gonna do with her little bit of money, but what she's really
gonna do is snort it or shoot it or eat it and it'll be gone. The
one person in a hundred who's not hooked on the damn stuff
is Maggie Boylan's husband. And what's he doing? He's setting
in that jail of ours. And the only reason her old man is sitting
in that jail is that Maggie was on parole and he took the rap for
her so she wouldn't have to go back to prison. And that's why I
gave her such a hard time back there on the highway. Now she's
off parole, but he's still in jail because . . . I don't know why he's
still in jail. It's his first charge ever, so he should have been out
long ago. But they're holding him for some reason, which I don't
know. My guess is they think they can pressure him to give her
up. But they don't know Gary."

He pulled the cruiser into the county parking lot and they
both got out. "You don't talk much, do you," Burke said.

Weatherstone nodded again. It was true.

"It's probably just as well. I talk enough for both of us. And I
probably talk more than I should." He leaned against the cruiser.
"I don't know why I told you all this. Sheriff already thinks I

took Maggie's ten dollars, but he can't prove it. If I hear you've passed it on, I'll call you seven kinds of a liar. Of course, it won't do me any good. He's trying to get rid of me anyway. I just got two years to retirement, but I know I won't make it that long. Do you want to know how I know?"

He did, but the deputy didn't wait for him to say so.

"You remember how the sheriff went to Portsmouth to recruit you for this job? Of course, you do. He knew you were a local boy and he saw you got good grades and he knew you would work hard and do what you're told. And being new, you come cheaper than us old dinosaurs. The county's hurting for money and they can't hold on to everybody. We got at least one more deputy than the budget will allow. So do the math and see what you get. Somebody's got to go. Somebody's in his sights. And who do you think it's gonna be? The old expensive, lazy one? Or the cheap young guy trying to make a name for himself?

"I reckon I'll find me a little trailer like that old man."

❖ ❖ ❖

THE SHERIFF paired Weatherstone with each of the deputies in turn, which meant that he covered all three shifts in the first week and in the second week as well. He looked every day at the older deputies on the force, who were, to a man, heavy in the gut, stiff in the bones, and slow. And he thought, will I be like them? He wanted to stay more like the lean, foxlike sheriff, whose campaign posters were still, a year after the election, stapled to trees and telephone poles every few miles along the main roads and even on some of the side roads. So once a day, every day, he ran the five miles from his mother's house, past Maggie Boylan's and back. He ran in daylight and in dark and he ran sometimes fresh and sometimes so worn and disoriented after doubled shifts that he ran himself right into a ditch.

But if ever he wavered, he had only to look to the posters, six or eight of them on the trees and poles along his path, to see the sheriff, faded, but still smiling, still looking lean, fit, and electable.

❖ ❖ ❖

AT ONE week into the job, Deputy Timothy Weatherstone made his first arrest. The sheriff had sent him in the cruiser out into the county to serve another notice. On his way back to town he saw an SUV parked along the side of the road and the driver slumped over the wheel.

Passed out, as it turned out. Weatherstone roused the driver, breathalyzed him, put him through the DUI paces, then read him his rights. "Wait a minute," the driver said. "My car wasn't even moving."

"Procedure, sir. Left wrist please." He waited for the man to raise his hand and then cuffed him.

"Now, wait a minute," the man said. "Do you know who I am?"

"I have all your information."

"No, I mean, do you *know* who I am?"

He did not. But when he got to the office with his prisoner, Tom Burke took one look and said, "Son, you've stepped in it now."

❖ ❖ ❖

AS IT turned out, Weatherstone's prisoner was a county judge.

"I understand," the judge told the sheriff. "He was just doing his job."

The judge nodded all around with a special nod to Deputy Weatherstone. "I appreciate your diligence, deputy."

"Yes, sir, thank you, sir," he said.

"Your mother was a fine woman."

"Thank you, sir. I thought so too."

"Keep up the good work."

"Yes, sir."

With one more general nod, the judge was out the door.

The sheriff tapped Weatherstone at the elbow, guided him into his office, and closed the door. "The judge is a diabetic," he said. "And diabetics sometimes get woozy. He pulled himself over to measure his sugar, but then he passed out. You caught him when he was just coming to."

"But sir, the breathalyzer . . ."

"The breathalyzer was defective."

"Sir, with all due respect . . ."

"It was defective, son. I tested it."

"Can you show me where it went wrong?"

"It's gone, son. I pitched it and the janitor came in and took the trash." The sheriff stared at Weatherstone in a way that almost dared him to look toward the trash can.

"That was an off-brand. We'll get a better one to replace it."

"Yes, sir."

"But you did the right thing. You followed procedure. There's a procedure on the books, so just follow procedure. If I could get the rest of this department to follow procedure, I'd be a happy man." He paused and looked to his watch, then continued. "So, do we understand each other, deputy?"

"I believe we do, sir."

The sheriff nodded toward the door and Deputy Weatherstone knew it was time to leave the office.

"You'll learn a little more about these things as you go along."

"Yes, sir."

"And by the way, Tom Burke is a little rough around the edges, but he's been a good deputy in his time. You could learn a lot from him."

"I'll try, sir."

"But don't listen to everything."

"No, sir."

"You're doing a good job, deputy."

"Thank you, sir."

"You can go now."

"Yes, sir." He stepped out into the outer office.

Burke was at the desk, pecking statistics into a computer. "So you got taken to the woodshed," he said.

Weatherstone glared and did not speak.

❖ ❖ ❖

FOUR DAYS later, the sky was a bright bolt of blue. But Burke was in a dark mood. He pulled shut the door to the sheriff's office, snatched the keys out of the desk, and said to Weatherstone,

"Come on, we got to set out that old man." The tenth day had come and gone and the old man had not come to court.

"So where's he gonna go?" Weatherstone asked.

"Not our problem," the deputy said. "If he's smart, he's already gone."

In the cruiser, Burke gripped the steering wheel as if he was trying to strangle it.

Weatherstone asked, "Are you all right?"

"I'm all right. I just want to know what in the hell made us want to become deputies in the first place? We could have been doctors or farmers or drug dealers or just about anything. So what were we thinking?" He looked to Weatherstone. "Out of all the things you could have been, why a small-town cop? Why a deputy in the Morris County Sheriff's Department? Did you watch too much TV?"

"We didn't have a TV."

"Your mother didn't believe in it, did she?"

Weatherstone glared. "Did you know my mother?"

"Son, everybody in this county, if they don't know somebody, they know somebody that knows them."

"But did you know my mother?"

"No," the deputy said. "I can't say as I did."

"Then don't talk about her."

They drove in silence for another mile. Finally, Weatherstone said, "I didn't get here from watching TV and it wasn't all about learning from books, like you seem to think. I'd like to help somebody the way some people helped me. Which you don't seem to understand."

"No," Burke said. "I don't reckon I do."

❖ ❖ ❖

WHY, TIMOTHY Weatherstone wondered, had that old man spotted him as Jenny Weatherstone's boy? He knew that was just the way people talked and that he would be, to those who knew her, Jenny Weatherstone's boy until the last of them died, but still, he hated being called a boy in front of Burke and he hated that everyone seemed to know his mother and her history better than he did.

For he remembered nothing of the time before his mother found the church. He knew, from hearing his mother testify, that she had been wild and had run with a wild crowd, that his older brother and sister had been sent to live with relatives in the city, that his father was a biker who died in a gunfight and that his mother had found Jesus and turned her life around.

But nothing before.

He had a recurring memory, which intruded into dream: He and his mother sat together on the worn benches of a country church: a young preacher snarled and sang his way through a sermon. "You might not like me here!" the preacher called. "But you'll like me in heaven." And the young preacher sang and he snarled until something in the sermon raised his mother, by the rhythmic snarl and song of it, up out of her seat, singing and clapping her hands. He must have been five, six years old and he was afraid his mother would spin away from him altogether, called into a joy that had never called him. He reached to grab her by the elbow and pull her back down, but she was gone down front to testify and left him alone on the bench.

❖ ❖ ❖

THE OLD man was not on his front step this time. The door of his trailer was open and Timothy Weatherstone expected to see him appear in the door as they pulled into the drive. But he didn't appear and he didn't answer Burke's call nor Weatherstone's knock.

Weatherstone stepped to the porch and peered in the doorway, but Burke stood back. "Do you see anything in there?"

"No sign." He knocked and called and got no answer. "Should I go in?"

"You can, but I don't think he's in there."

Weatherstone stepped through the door and into the trailer. He called the old man's name again and the name fell like lead. There was not a breath of sound. The fire had gone out of the wood stove. On top of the stove, a skillet with a gray pool of bacon grease. On the kitchen table, a plate with the cold remains of a breakfast. In the bedroom, bathroom—still nothing.

Outside, Burke studied the woodpile. "Hasn't been touched," he said. "Not since we were out here ten days ago." He looked over to the porch. "And the water jugs, check them out. There's not a one of them out of place."

"So where is he?"

"Not far, I don't reckon."

Burke's hunch took them out to the edge of the pasture. They found him—the picked-over, pillaged rags and bones of him—in a scattered half circle at the cliff edge. "Buzzards by day, coyotes by night," Burke said. "It ain't pretty." The old man's hat, coat, boots, and the shotgun that had probably done the deed, were scattered out with him. A few scraps of him lay in the sand and gravel at the bottom of the cliff. Either they had fallen as the dozers undermined the bank or the buzzards had cast them down as refuse.

The deputy shook his head. "You can see what kind of help we were to this old bird."

❖ ❖ ❖

THEY REMAINED on the scene for several hours more. They had to call off the trucks and dozers from working under the cliff and scraping up any more remnants of the man. They cordoned off the area with crime scene tape, called in the county coroner and the forensics from Portsmouth, photographed each site, and canvassed each clump of dusty Johnson grass or ironweed for any bit of nightmare bone. By the end of it, they had most of him— the stripped bones, a few hanks of hair and scalp, his boots, some torn, bloody rags of his clothing, and a few fragments of teeth and his broken, blown-out skull—all stacked in a grisly pile near the shotgun which they had dusted for prints. "He probably used a deer slug," Burke said. "You wouldn't want bird shot for a job like this."

At the end of it, long after dark, the forensics bagged the old man up and took him away.

❖ ❖ ❖

WHEN BURKE and Weatherstone got back to the office, there was still the report to write. "You're the one with the college education," Burke said. He threw the keys in the desk drawer and walked out. So Weatherstone got the job of typing up the report, which proceeded to detail their discovery of the remains of the alleged victim, assumed to be the individual named in the Notice to Vacate and stated that they were unable, due to the scattered condition of said remains, to make a positive identification, but noted the similarity to the above individual's clothing, including hat, shoes, coat, shirt, and trousers when seen on the previous date, and then to detail the steps taken to secure the area and to contact forensics and to assist the forensics and the coroner after they arrived, and noted that, coroner's report pending, there was no immediate evidence to suggest foul play and that the likely cause of death was suicide.

He reviewed the report, decided it said what he wanted it to say, printed it out, put it on the sheriff's desk, and drove himself home.

He ran that night harder than he had ever run. And still, his sleep was haunted with rag and bone.

❖ ❖ ❖

IT WAS by now mid-December. The hour had fallen back and darkness fell each night with a suddenness and finality that caught Timothy Weatherstone by surprise. So now, when he ran, it was almost always after dark. But he always took the same near-memorized path, down the road and along the creek and back.

The moon was at the half and it half-lit the creek and the hills around him. He ran down the road past Maggie Boylan's little house. There was a couch on the porch with an afghan laid across it and all looked normal and neighborly. But none of Maggie's house lights were on, just a security light for the yard, and he guessed that Maggie was across the creek getting her fix. A car came up the road and he trotted into Maggie's drive to let it pass. The car had a low-pitched rumble running through its pipes and a high-pitched guitar riffing through its speakers. Here comes another one, he thought. He watched the taillights cross over the rattling bridge and climb the gravel lane to the top of Pillhead Hill.

"We're just waiting till the time is right," the sheriff had said. "We've got undercover working." He trusted the sheriff, but each night, the cars rolled down the road, steadily, one after another; and this car with its rumble and riff would be followed soon by yet another.

He ran on, keeping to a path between the road and the creek. Beyond Maggie Boylan's, there was a bend in the road and Maggie's was the last lighted house. So, past the bend, he ran strictly by moonlight and memory. The rumble and the radio and the voices from the house on the hill faded. Soon there was only the pound of his shoes on the pavement and, in another half-mile, as the pavement ran out, the scratch of his shoes on the gravel.

He ran at times by the feel of it. He knew that the gravel was loose in one place and pounded into rock dust in another. He knew the road ran smooth in one place and rutted in another and he felt how the road banked at the curve and where it dipped and where it rose and where it ran straight and where it swerved. So he was not prepared when solid ground turned suddenly to water. The first splashy step startled him, but it was five, six, a dozen steps more before he could come to a slow, cold, shin-deep stop.

He looked around and saw nothing that he recognized. It was dark water all around him, the ripples glinting here and there in the half-moon light. A rippling image of the half-moon floated in the middle of the pool whose surface was broken by trees, floating branches, and spikes of fescue and Johnson grass. He had gotten deep enough and had turned himself sufficiently around, that he could no longer tell which way he had come in nor how to get out. A telephone pole rose from the middle of the pool. Stapled to it was the smiling poster image of the sheriff. Weatherstone stood and faced the sheriff a moment, and tried to recall where that pole stood along his path. But the sheriff was no help to him.

It made no sense. There had been no recent rain, no word of a flood downstream. He started to shiver from the cold.

In a moment, he heard a shimmer to his left. A black line crossed the moon-bright tablet of the water: a beaver, still at work on her dam. She paused, curious, gazed at him a moment, then dove with a gunshot flap of her tail and was gone.

❖   ❖   ❖

IN HIS second week, Timothy Weatherstone was scheduled for the long dull hours of a rainy overnight at the jail. The rain was a silent, steady, daylong, nightlong rain that tapped at the windows and showed no sign of letting up. He talked for a while to an old bootlegger, checked on the dozen or so others, and when it was lights out, quiet set in. There were rounds to do every hour or so, the radio, a paperback novel, a look into the Bible someone had left, some filing, another check of the cells, a pot of coffee brewed, a frozen pizza microwaved, then coffee, radio, a cheap magazine, every word of the local paper.

Bored with it all, desperate to stay awake, with hours to go before the end of this endless shift, he paced the office floor, did pushups, squats, and jumping jacks, then settled back into the paperback book.

Along about two in the morning, he heard a voice from out in the street and went to the window. A woman stood on the sidewalk across the street. Her head was bare, her rain-blackened hair streamed to her shoulders. Her shoulders had huddled in for warmth and her rain-soaked jacket sagged. She raised her pale face to look up at the jailhouse windows and called out a name. Weatherstone could not make out the name she called. It could have been any of the names in his cells. No one answered and she shivered and called out again. Two more times and she turned to walk away and Weatherstone heard a voice from down the corridor—her man, one of the men in his jail—had wakened to her voice and had answered her.

There was a stir and a mumble from the others, but no one complained. Man and woman shouted back and forth for nearly five minutes. Weatherstone knew he was supposed to break it up, but he hesitated. Maybe they would stop on their own. And sure enough, the woman waved and the shouting stopped. She wiped her eyes, then waved one more time and was gone.

❖ ❖ ❖

THE RAIN continued to fall through the night and into the morning, steady and relentless, all day and into the next. Weatherstone finished his rainy overnight shift, drove home through the fog and rain, and slept for a few droning hours before he came back to work at three in the afternoon for a second shift that he spent catching speeders with a radar gun. He had to double that shift, because one of the other deputies was down with the flu and another was stuck on the wrong side of a washed-out road. So he spent a second night watching over the jailhouse and listening to the rain. Toward midnight, the rain slowed, then stopped, only to start again with the same diluvian persistence.

Again, at the same hour, the black-haired woman stood in the rain and called up to her man. And again, by the rules, he knew he should put a stop to it, but could not bring himself to do it. For five minutes, maybe ten, they called to each other over the drumming rain. Then she left and all was quiet until just before dawn when the sheriff relieved him and sent him home.

He hung a blanket over his window to block the foggy daylight and the sound of the rain and he slept like the dead.

❖ ❖ ❖

HE WOKE by midafternoon, so refreshed and so restless from all the residual caffeine still hammering in his blood, that he took a notion to drive into town and pick up his check—his first check—and to pay some bills.

The rain had stopped sometime in the morning and a steady wind had driven most of the clouds to the east. Sunlight glinted in the flooded furrows and in the choked ditches. The creeks had backed up into the low ground and cattle in the feedlots

stood ankle deep in the glittering muck. The calves, never having
known such brightness, blinked and bawled.

❖   ❖   ❖

IT TOOK a moment for Weatherstone's eyes to adjust to the
dimness of the office, but he saw, once he could see, that Burke,
still in uniform, wore neither badge nor gun belt. He and
another deputy—a sergeant—stood over Burke's desk and on
the desk was a cardboard box.

"Well, son," Burke said. "I see you've come to my retirement
party. It don't look like much of a party, but it's the best I can do
for now."

Burke showed the sergeant a stack of books and the sergeant
nodded, so Burke put the books into the box.

Weatherstone went to his mail slot and pulled out his
check.

"I see you're starting to collect that county check," Burke
said. "You're getting your first and I'm getting my last and the
first shall be last and the last shall be first and that's the way it
goes." He saw the puzzlement in Weatherstone's eye and said,
"Oh, I don't reckon you know what's happening. See, your
buddy, the sheriff has informed me that my services are no
longer required by this department."

"You're leaving?"

"Not exactly on my own free will, but then you knew that."

Burke showed the sergeant a pen and a couple pencils, got
the sergeant's nod, threw them into the box, and started to fold
up the lid.

The sergeant looked to Weatherstone. "Can you wait here a
couple minutes? I got some paperwork to fetch." Weatherstone
nodded and the sergeant left the room.

"So tell me," Burke said. "Actually, you don't have to tell
me, but I'll ask anyway. Did you tell the sheriff about our episode
with Maggie?"

Weatherstone shook his head, ever so slightly, no. Then he
turned away.

"No? Well, that's good. I reckoned Sheriff had wormed it out of you. I figured you'd try to hold your ground, but he'll dig at you like a terrier does a mole."

The sheriff had, in fact, dug it out of him. But he had not had to dig hard. The sheriff asked and Weatherstone had told the story willingly, without hesitation. It had been wrong to take Maggie's money and so, he told. But still, he felt a wave of guilt. He tried to speak; he felt he should say something, but he could not think of what he could say. He knew it showed in his face, so he turned his face away.

But Burke had studied what showed in his face. "It's okay, son. You just did what you thought was right." The sergeant came back and passed him a paper across the desk. He signed it and passed it back. "He'd have got me one way or another."

Weatherstone nodded. He did not know what he could say.

"So don't worry about me," Burke said. "I'm gonna buy me a cheap banjo and set on the porch and pick till my social security kicks in."

He hoisted the box and the sergeant led him out the door and down the stairs.

❖ ❖ ❖

IN THOSE soggy, work-bound, housebound days when he had not been able to run, Timothy Weatherstone had started into something like withdrawal. He was tired when awake and restless when he slept and the echo of his footsteps in his near-empty house took him to the near side of crazy.

But now, the rains had stopped. The waters receded from the swales and the ditches and a farmer had busted up the beaver dam. So his path was clear; he could hear the pound of his feet on the pavement again and the scratch of his shoes on the gravel.

There was but a sliver of moon now and Weatherstone ran half-blind, relying on memory to keep him on his half-remembered path and free of any stumble-place or pothole likely to take out an ankle or wreck a knee. He ran his dark path, past Maggie Boylan and Pillhead Hill with its usual noise of music and voices and, once he hit the gravel, his nerves exulted in the bath of endorphins that flooded in with the miles.

He ran down past the wreckage of the beaver dam and made ready to turn around. Then, sudden as snakebite, he went down. He had stepped into a shadowy spot where the rains had guttered out the gravel and his ankle crumpled back on itself and pulled the props from under him and he was all of a sudden face down in the damp of rock and rock dust and sand. He raised himself up on his hands and waited. There was no pain at first, just a low feeling in the gut that was close to despair.

Jesus, he whispered, just let me walk. Just let me get to work tomorrow. Then, the pain washed through him and took all his brain away. He stifled a cry—he did not know why, for there was none to hear him cry—but in the next wave of pain he gave up a stream of curses so fluent and accomplished that he surprised himself with them. He cursed with enough animal energy to set half a dozen dogs barking up and down the holler road and the owls to booming in the woods to either side. He cursed himself up onto hands and knees and tried to stand and cursed himself back down when he could not stand and cursed around on the ground on the side of the road until he found a stick he could use to crutch himself up. He was at the farthest reach of his run, miles from home. He had no phone and the only cars on the road at this hour would be headed to Pillhead Hill to buy or to sell. His ankle throbbed him like a little naggy child. It was time to stop thinking and move. But he had no idea how to use a crutch. He put his toe to the gravel, tried to take a step, and went brainless again with the pain. He found, after a couple more painful tries, that he could grip the stick with both hands, plant it in the gravel, and hop forward on his good leg. So he cursed and crutched his cold, crippled way back up the road, past the abandoned farmhouses and the carcasses of barns, past the trees where the sheriff smiled from his poster. He had to stop twice to rest. Finally, he came around the bend and saw the lights from Maggie Boylan's house.

"Maggie," he called. It was too far away for her to hear, another hundred yards at least, but he called anyway. "Yo, Maggie," he called again. The owls hooted him back and the half-dozen dogs took up the chant again.

By now, his good leg had begun to tremble from exhaustion and the stick had begun to blister his hands. But he hop-walked all the faster, for once he got to Maggie's house, he would be able to rest. Maggie, who had known him as a child, would take him in and feed him and let him get warm and, he hoped, would let him use a phone.

He hobble-hopped up to her gate and through the gate and up her walk to the porch. He was drunk with pain and he was cold. "Maggie," he roared and the word roared back at him off the glass of Maggie's door.

"Maggie, are you there?"

She was not. With a string of final curses, he stumbled to the couch that was on the porch and collapsed upon it. He tucked his feet up under him, wrapped the afghan around him, and shivered himself to sleep.

He woke—somewhere in the night, an eagle of pain had lifted him out of his sleep—and there was Maggie Boylan in her old man's oversized coat. She had paused just across the road at the foot of the bridge, wondering, probably, who could it be on her porch?

"It's me," he called. "Tim Weatherstone."

He thought she would roll him out a carpet of curses. Instead, she nodded and started across the road, slow-stepping toward him with a glaze of perfect contentment across her eyes.

She stopped just short of the porch and peered. "Timmy?"

"Yeah, it's me, Timmy."

"What the fuck are you doing here?"

He told her the story and she nodded again. Then, moving slowly as if she were under water, she helped him into the house, set him down on a couch, packed the ankle with ice, heaped blankets around him, and brought him hot soup and a little white pill.

"What's this?"

"Don't ask. Just take the motherfucker."

He would have argued—he told himself he should argue; there were so many reasons to argue and so many things that could go wrong—but he had been shivered with pain for too long and he was weary and broken-willed, so he took the pill and washed it down with a slug of soup.

In just a moment, all seemed right, the most right it had ever been. The pain had moved to a place a hundred yards down the road; it was no longer his pain; it belonged to some other person who merely dressed like him and looked like him. The room around him seemed to sing; the blood rang in his ears like a tambourine. It seemed he was lifted from the couch and its warm nest of blankets into a wordlessly joyous space that delighted him and terrified him and which he did not want to leave. He looked around him; everything in the room had its own radiant life. And in the midst of all, sat Maggie Boylan, skinny and serene. Keeping watch with her nightingale eye, she looked just like the mother of all.

Liars

EDIE O'LEARY—her name was Edna, but everybody called her Edie—had lived so close to the bone that, even now, at two years sober, she looked to be all bone herself, lean as a rib, sinewy and intense.

It was January and there was a bitter, January wind, but she was aching for a cigarette so she was out on the front steps of the Square Deal Grill. It was the middle of the morning rush and there was no one else to work the booths or the counter. The best she could do was to fire up a quick one. She had just time enough to suck down three shivering hits and to see, across the courthouse square, Deputy Tim Weatherstone, stringing yellow crime scene tape across the front of the drugstore.

Three hits on her cigarette, that was all, and she had to get back to work. No one said anything—they all knew better than to say anything. But she could sense six pairs of eyes at her back and a worried cook in the kitchen. Someone's order was ready; someone wanted his check; the caffeine level in the room was growing critical.

She stabbed her cigarette out against the doorframe, then carefully inserted the half-cigarette back into its pack, dropped the pack into her apron pocket, and came back inside to catch the order, refill the depleted coffee cups, and fetch that bill.

"What do you reckon happened over at the drugstore?" one old farmer at the counter asked another.

"I have no idea," the second farmer said.

Edie O'Leary had an idea, but she kept her idea to herself.

The two farmers shrugged and continued to watch out the front door and across the courthouse lawn to where the yellow tape fluttered. By now, the sheriff and a state trooper had arrived to ponder the broken door and the glass on the sidewalk.

"Do you reckon it was a break-in?" the first old farmer asked.

"Probably was."

"There's a lot of that going around."

"I hear there is."

"Ever drugstore in ever little town from here to Gallipolis has been hit."

"That's right."

"And over in Kentucky, it's just as bad."

"That's what they say."

"And you don't dare leave your house, they'll strip it to the bare walls."

"That they will."

"Used to be you never had to lock your door."

"Never did."

"Ain't like that no more. Ask me why, I say it's the drugs. It makes them crazy."

"It does."

"Makes them so crazy for it they'll do about anything to get more."

"Bout anything."

"It makes you wonder just what is this world coming to."

"Makes you think."

❖ ❖ ❖

EDIE O'LEARY did not have much time to think while she was at work. And she liked it like that. In the one slack hour between the breakfast run and the lunch rush, with nothing to occupy her mind and hands, it was too easy to let stress, worry, and regret invade her mind.

So she was grateful when Tim Weatherstone came in, wearing his new county uniform, starched so stiff it looked like armor and pressed so sharp it could have been registered as a weapon. He was young and he walked with a young man's strut and he swaggered with a young man's swagger. But Edie O'Leary had known him since he was a boy.

No, she told him, she hadn't seen a thing. Yes, she got to work at five in the morning, but she wasn't looking at such an hour to see whose windows were broken, so no, she didn't see a thing, and no, she didn't hear a thing, and no, she didn't know a thing until she saw the yellow tape, so that by the time Weatherstone left, she was no longer grateful to have seen him at all and she was reminded of way too many times she had to answer way too many questions.

So she was only half grateful to see Maggie Boylan headed toward the door of the Square Deal with Sheila Hacker by the elbow. Maggie steered Sheila up the steps and through the door.

"Come on, babe," Maggie said. "Edie'll front us some coffee. That'll help your nerves."

Maggie marched the girl to the counter and planted her on a stool. "Edie's my old running dog," said Maggie. "She's sober now, but she's not stuck-up sober like some." Sheila was younger than Maggie and Edie by ten or fifteen years and she was tagged with initials on her hands and studded with metal rings in her lip and brow. She placed her hands flat on the counter, looked to the window, and bit her lip.

"She's worried, because she thinks they're gonna charge her for the break-in at the drugstore. But I told her, don't worry, I got your back."

The girl looked out to the window and shook her head. She hunched her shoulders up and pulled her head down into the collar of her coat and tongued the ring in her lip.

"She's all shook up and nervous and she needs a cup of coffee," Maggie said.

"Maggie, I can't give you coffee every time you drag yourself in here."

Maggie looked to the girl. "You see how she talks to me?" She gave Edie a look. "I ain't asking for me. It's for her."

The girl's hands did not move from the counter, but they shimmered, leaf-like. Her knuckles were red and her nails were bitten to the nub.

Edie poured coffee for the girl and one for Maggie and thought, This is trouble in the making.

"They got it in for me," the girl said. "I know they do. They got no one else they can blame, so they're gonna try to pin it on me."

"So I'll just tell them, you was with me all last night."

"But what if . . ."

"What if what?"

"I don't know. I just know they're gonna try to put it on me."

"Don't worry, babe. I got you covered."

Edie O'Leary rapped once on the counter. "Maggie," she said. "Come back here a second." She marched Maggie to the back booth and sat her down. "I don't know what you're trying to do with that girl," she said, "but I see a truckload of trouble coming."

"She's just a kid," Maggie said. "I'm trying to help her out."

"You're gonna help yourself right into a jail cell."

"Somebody's got to help her."

"By telling the cops some kind of bullshit lie? Look, suppose she did it—which, if she did, I don't want to know about it—but if she did and you're trying to stand in the way, well, there you go. You might as well put your hands out for the cuffs. And if she didn't do it, what the hell does she need you for?"

"I'm telling you, she's just a kid. She don't know how to handle these things."

"And you do? Maggie, it's not that long since you handled yourself a year in Marysville."

"I knew you was gonna throw that in my face."

"I didn't throw it in your face."

"Then why did you even bring it up?"

"Because you always seem to forget it."

"How am I supposed to forget going to prison and losing my kids?"

"I don't reckon you ever will, but do you ever want to get them back?"

"Are you saying I'm unfit too?"

"I'm saying. . . ." She took a deep breath for patience. "I'm saying that you're putting yourself in a bad place."

"Because I want to help that girl? I thought you was better than that."

"Maggie . . ."

"Used to be you would help somebody like her."

"Maggie, I'm trying to help you."

"Help, my ass. I thought you was my friend."

"You can think what you want, Maggie." Edie O'Leary was done with patience now. "I got to get back to work."

Two secretaries from the courthouse had sat down at the counter. The girl stared out the door.

"Come on," Maggie called to her. "They don't want the likes of us in here." She grabbed the girl by the elbow and pressed her out into the street. A feed mill truck had to hit the brakes to keep from turning them into mulch. The driver honked and Maggie waved him the bird. Maggie talked the girl around the corner and out of sight and she was gone.

Soon, everyone was gone. The secretaries took their coffees back to the courthouse; the old farmers paid up and went their way. The cook came up front to say that everything was ready and he would be back before lunch. So she was alone with her thoughts. She busied herself with filling the saltshakers and the napkin holders, but really, there was nothing to do until the first of the lunch crowd came around. To keep the old thoughts cornered, she threw on a sweater and went back out to the step to smoke. She came back in, all ashiver, dialed her sponsor, and left a voice mail. She wiped the counter clean and polished the racks that held the menus. Everything was as clean as she could make it.

❖ ❖ ❖

LATER, AFTER the lunch rush was over, there were still some customers in no big hurry. The old farmers had been replaced by a new set of old farmers and a new set of courthouse secretaries sat talking in a booth. Six or seven others were scattered among the other booths or at the counter. There was plenty to do now, so Edie O'Leary did not notice right away that Sheila Hacker sat at the counter, close by the register, with her hands flat on the table. She was nibbling at the ring in her lip and staring out across the courthouse square.

"Can I get you something, honey?"

"Can I just sit here?"

"Honey, it's a restaurant."

The girl looked left and right, then pressed her hands even tighter to the countertop, so Edie turned on her heel, poured a cup of coffee, set the cup in front of the girl and asked, "Are you hungry?"

"I didn't bring my purse."

"Hold on," said Edie. She went back to the kitchen, pulled out a plate, and prepped an order of the meat loaf special. She set it in front of the girl and went on about her business. The secretaries were ready for their bill, the new old farmers wanted pie, and the half dozen others wanted some of this or some of that. When she finally got back to the girl, she had her fork in hand, but she had not eaten more than a nibble off the corner of the meatloaf and had barely put a dent into the mashed potatoes.

"You all right, honey?"

"I'm just nervous, is all."

"They ain't charged you yet, honey. I wouldn't worry about it."

The girl pondered this a moment. She looked up, nibbled at the ring in her in her lip, then asked, "How did you do it?"

"Do what, honey?"

"How did you get clean? How did you get off the drugs?"

Edie looked around. No one else was listening. It was an opening, a chance to carry the message. She leaned closer. "Honey, they court-ordered me to treatment," she said. "Or else

I probably would still be out there. Or dead. I lost my kids and everything, just like Maggie. But I'd probably still be out there."

The girl nodded, but she kept one eye on the door.

"It worked, but I had to let it work."

The girl drummed her fingers on the counter. She looked again to the window.

"The court got me in the door. But I had to want it more than I wanted to get high."

One of the new old farmers raised his coffee mug to catch Edie's eye. Edie glared him down.

"Cause if you don't want it," she said to the girl, "it's not gonna happen. First couple times I went to rehab, I didn't really want it. I still wanted to party. They tried to tell me what was up, but I wasn't listening. I couldn't wait to get out and get high again. I knew the OxyContin was eating me alive, but I didn't care. But this last time . . ."

The girl interrupted. "I heard you was the one to get Maggie Boylan started on Oxy."

"Who told you that?"

The girl looked away.

"Okay," Edie said. "It don't matter." She thought for a moment. If she knows that, what else does she know?

The old farmer had raised his cup again and the secretaries had risen and were headed for the register.

"Hold on, babe," Edie said. She rang up the secretaries and took their money. She poured the farmer's refill, cleared the secretaries' table, and scooped up their morsel of a tip. She hesitated a moment before she turned back to the girl. After all, she thought, if I got Maggie started on Oxy and Maggie got the girl started, which was likely, then I've got a hand in whatever happens from here on out. The thought was as troublesome as any she had ever had. So she busied herself with bussing the tables. She carried the dishes back to the kitchen, said her short prayer, and came back out to face the girl.

But the girl was gone. Quick as that, the girl was gone.

❖   ❖   ❖

AT TWO in the afternoon, the new old farmers were still in place, each of them working through a third or fourth refill. A couple of teenagers skipping school, a couple truckers on a break—that was all. Everyone was talking quietly, one of the old farmers might tell a joke and the other one laugh, but for half an hour, it had been quiet as the moments before church.

It was quiet enough to set Edie O'Leary to thinking again: It's a hard thing, she thought, to set a thing right once you've set it wrong. For Maggie Boylan had always been a wild one, but she had never been so wild and never so lost and devious, never so spare of flesh and so all out at the bones before Edie O'Leary, high and heedless, had shared with her that first OxyContin.

And then Maggie Boylan herself blew in the door. She marched straight up to Edie and pounded a bony fist on the counter.

"Where is she?"

"You mean that girl you brought in?"

"I mean that little metalmouth bitch that, yes I brought her in here this morning, and I need to know where the hell she went."

"I don't know, but Maggie, I told you I saw trouble coming."

"Well, there's gonna be more trouble soon as I find her. If I can catch her before a cop catches me, that'll be the end of it right there."

"Maggie, what is up with you? One minute you're willing to go to jail for the girl and the next you want to kill her."

"What's up with her is what you need to ask."

"So what's up with her?"

"That sheriff scared her good enough that she decided to give me up so they'd let her go. So she ratted me out, that's what happened. She flat-out lied on me. She told the cops I did that break-in. And now they're looking for me."

"Maggie, you lie down with dogs . . ."

"I know, you get up with fleas. So tell me what happened to that particular fleabag bitch I'm looking for."

"She left here about an hour ago."

"Which way?"

"Maggie, I don't know. I looked up and she was here and I looked away and she was gone."

One of the new old farmers pointed out the front door of the Grill. "She went left out the door looking like a scared rabbit."

"She ought to be scared," Maggie said. She turned to leave.

"Maggie," Edie said.

"I ain't got time," Maggie said. "I got to stop this little lying bitch." She slammed the door behind her and started up the street to the left.

❖ ❖ ❖

AT THREE in the afternoon, Edie O'Leary told the old farmers, "I've been here ten hours without a break and I'm ready to go home."

The cook was on his way out the door and the owner was on his way in. Edie called to him, "Stavros, when you gonna get me some help in here?"

"You find somebody who will do the job," he said in his heavy Greek accent. She started to bus the plates from the truckers, but Stavros said, "Put it down. I got it from here."

Edie did not argue. She counted up her tips and left the cook his share, then gathered her purse, sweater, and jacket. She took out a cigarette and her lighter and had the cigarette on her lips as she came out the door and onto the steps. She paused on the front step to light up the cigarette and let the nicotine massage her troubled nerves. She exhaled and let the wind take the smoke away. It was a January wind with the bitterness of a January wind and it carried with it the sound of voices from across the square. The words were baffled and rendered half-unreadable by the gusts, but she recognized them as curses and she recognized the voice as the voice of Maggie—oh my God, she thought—crazy Maggie Boylan with her hands cuffed behind her, her eyes narrow with rage, Tim Weatherstone at one arm and another deputy at the other and to the side, the sheriff himself, watching like the smug sonofabitch that he was.

At a word from the sheriff, the deputies began to steer Maggie toward the jailhouse on the other side of the square, but five steps in, Maggie balked and would not be budged. She glared toward the courthouse steps and her curses suddenly became more urgent and precise. For coming down the courthouse steps was Sheila Hacker. For just a moment, Sheila stood, struck deer-blind by Maggie and her curses. But quickly she spat out a string of curses of her own, turned, and scuttled back into the courthouse.

The deputies found their traction and dragged Maggie away. But still, she cursed. She cursed the girl and her lie. She cursed the deputies right and left. She cursed her luck and the day she was born. She cursed the whole world around her until they shoved her through the jailhouse door.

Edie O'Leary dropped the butt of her cigarette and crushed it under her toe. The others from around the square who had been watching now turned to talk with each other. In a moment, the wind drove them all off the square and Edie O'Leary was left alone in the cold to trouble out what she had once set wrong and now could never set right.

All This Craziness

COREY HACKER leaned out over her porch rail and peered once more up the road and into the dark.

"She'll come home when she wants to come home," her husband said from the door. "Come on in before you catch your death of cold."

"Hush," she said. "Wait a minute." Her voice was sharp. Sharper than she intended, but there it was. She was lean as an axe handle and her eye was sharp as her words. She cut him a look with the blade of her eye, hoping he would back off.

"Let her go," he said. "She's grown."

"She's not grown."

"She's twenty-two years old. She's grown. She can do what she wants. I did what I wanted when I was twenty-two. And so did you."

And look where it got us, she wanted to say. Donald was a preacher now, but he had been in a biker gang when he was younger and he had the scars and the tattoos and the crooked-leg limp to prove it. She had left her first husband for this man and his tattoos—the scars and the crushed leg came later. She remembered that and took her sharp eye away.

"She's still a baby to me," she said.

"She had her own mind when she was a baby," he said. "Even before all this craziness."

Craziness: Sheila, her daughter, her only, her hope and her heart, the child of her own crazy youth. The girl had taken to running the roads late of a night, making all the wrong decisions with all the wrong people, running afoul of the law and good sense. She had dropped the college scholarship and picked up the wild boyfriend, the wild moods, the tattoos and the piercings, and the OxyContin, the crazy cause of it all.

"I thought she quit for good this time," her mother said. "I really thought for sure she would quit."

"You don't need to wait out here anyway," Donald said. "You'll hear that muffler long before you see any headlights."

"In and out of treatment, how many times? In and out of jail? You'd think she would have learned from all we went through. And now this business of testifying against her so-called best friend. You'd think," she said. "You'd think she'd start to see it."

He said nothing to that. He held the door open and waited.

She noticed the silence and thought, he knows something and he's not about to say it. It set her to pondering in the backyard of her mind.

She peered over the porch rail one more time, then followed him into the house. He was right; it was the dead of night, it was the dead of winter. It was too late, too cold to be watching for a set of headlights that might not come at all.

He told her goodnight and limped off to bed. "I'll be up directly," she told him. She had to be at work first thing; she needed to get some sleep. But first, she settled into a kitchen chair. She loosened her hair from its clips and bands. She took a brush from the pocket of her gown and began to brush her hair. It fell nearly to the floor and she brushed it out and brushed it out and then put the hairbrush down, pulled her hair back, divided it into three strands, then wove the strands into a long, thick braid.

He knows something, she thought. He's been talking to that courthouse crowd and he knows something but he won't say what he knows.

And she would have asked, but by the time she came to bed, her husband had fallen asleep with his Bible collapsed in front of him and his big hands splayed out like fallen pillars.

❖ ❖ ❖

SHE SLEPT, but she did not sleep long. At some time before
dawn, she heard the ragged rumble of the muffler coming down
the road and up the drive, then a shuffle and a stumble and a
whisper of voices and she got up to check.

Sheila and her wild boyfriend stood in her bedroom in front
of her dresser, stuffing clothes and cosmetics into a duffel. A
backpack and a spangled purse, already filled, waited by the door.
They were working in the light of a small study lamp. So when
Corey turned on the overhead light, they both stood startled,
half blind, and blinking.

"What the f—!" The boyfriend saw who it was and broke off.

Her daughter did not. "Ma! What the fuck? Are you trying
to blind us?"

"What's going on?"

"Can you tell?"

"It looks like you're packing to leave."

"That's exactly what I'm doing."

"Your dad'll not be happy."

"Donald's not my dad."

"He'll do till you find you a better one."

"I got to go, Ma. Maggie Boylan's gonna kick my ass if she
sees me."

"She's gonna see you at five in the morning?"

"Not yet, but she will."

"Because you testified against her?"

"She's trying to say I lied on her."

"Did you?"

"Did I what?"

"Did you tell a lie on Maggie Boylan?"

"Did Donald tell you I did?"

"He never said a word. I just want to know. Did you lie on
Maggie Boylan?"

"Ma, I can't believe you're even asking me such a thing."

"Did you?" The notion had festered and now she needed
to know.

"I'm not going through this all over again."

"All I did was ask. And you can't give me a straight answer. That says a lot."

"It says I'm tired of you and your nosy questions."

"As long as you're living under my roof, I got a right to an answer."

"Ma, I got to go. Maggie's looking for me. And when I'm gone, you can keep your roof for yourself."

"Donald's here. He's not gonna let you come to any harm."

"Donald's gonna say, let her suffer the natural consequences."

"Maggie Boylan's not a natural consequence."

"No, she's a natural disaster and I got to get out of the way."

Corey nodded toward the boyfriend. "You got all the disaster you need right there. He's a one-man catastrophe."

"Ma, don't start." She emptied the last drawer into the duffel and hitched it to her shoulder.

"Let me see your eyes," Corey said. "I want to see does he have you on something."

"Ma, I'm not your little girl anymore."

"Let me see your eyes."

"Ma, no."

The mother squinted up her own eyes to see better. She even turned the beam of the study lamp on her daughter's face. "Let me see," she said. Her word and eye were sharp again.

"Come on, Ronnie, we got to get out of here," the daughter said.

The woman stepped to block her daughter's path.

"Ma! Have you gone totally crazy?"

The boyfriend looked from mother to daughter with eyes big as dollar coins.

"Corey, let her go." Donald was limping down the hall.

"Ma, I swear. If you don't get out of the way, I'm gonna knock you right down the stairs."

"I want to see your eyes."

"Let her go," Donald said. "Just let her pass."

"Do what he says, Ma. For once in your life, do the sensible thing."

Her husband took her by the shoulder and started to guide her backward out of their path.

She didn't fight him; she knew she had lost this battle long ago.

"Go on," Corey said. "There's nothing ever gonna be right in this world. You might as well be wrong with the rest."

"This is crazy," said the daughter. "This whole family is crazy."

"If you leave," the mother said, "you ain't coming back."

"If I leave, you're right. I'm not ever coming back. I don't want to ever come back to this crazy house."

Corey started to flare back; the words were right at the gate of her teeth. But she knew there was nothing more to say. She let her husband pull her back further down the hall. Sheila and Ronnie lifted the duffle and the backpack and trundled them down the stairs.

Corey turned away. She shrugged her husband's hands off her shoulders and stared away where she could not see them leave.

They stood in the hall for several long minutes as the girl and her boyfriend stumbled their plunder down the steps. They heard the trundle-thump at each step, then the creak of the porch boards, and the throaty roar of Sheila's perforated muffler as they scratched and rumbled out the drive and down the road.

"I thought you was gonna fix that muffler," the mother said.

"There's a lot of things I ain't yet fixed," he said. They stood in the dark hall and talked of mufflers and rain gutters and all manner of things in need of fixing.

They spoke in a hush, at a bare whisper, though there really was no need.

Probation

MAGGIE BOYLAN sat in her place and glared at the judge as hard a glare as she dared to give. But her glare was nothing to the judge. He kept his eyes on the papers laid out on the bench and he nodded as the lawyers—her lawyer on one side and the prosecutor on the other—said those things that lawyers say when they're deciding someone's case.

Finally, at a word from the judge, Maggie's lawyer nodded to the prosecutor and the prosecutor nodded to the judge and the judge wrote something on the papers and the little circle of men broke up.

Her lawyer sat back down beside her. He shrugged. "We got as good a deal as we're gonna get," he whispered.

She whispered back, "Did you get me off?"

"Maggie, I pulled out everything I had, but God himself couldn't have got you off this one."

"I didn't pay God to be my lawyer."

"If it comes to that, you didn't pay me either. The county pays my tab, for what it's worth."

"Well, what did the county get for its money?"

"The judge'll tell us in just a minute."

"Cooper, I swear I didn't do it."

"You can swear all you want. They had a witness."

"And that witness lied."

"But the judge believed her."

"I told you we should of gone for a jury trial."

"Maggie, there's not twelve people in this county you haven't pissed off."

"I ain't gonna go back to prison."

"There's not twelve people in this county that haven't caught you in a lie."

"There's nothing on earth gonna make me go back to Marysville."

"I've caught you in a few lies myself."

"I'll hide out in the hills. I'll live off of squirrel meat and raw grass."

"Hush, Maggie." He tapped her arm and pointed to the bench.

"I'm telling you, I ain't gonna go back to prison."

"Maggie, hush."

She would have given him a hush-my-ass, but the bucket-blue eye of the judge glared her into silence. He glared her so hard, she felt she had been nailed to the back of her seat.

The bailiff called out, "The defendant will now rise."

Cooper stood, but Maggie could not rise until the judge lowered his gaze and looked back down to his papers.

❖   ❖   ❖

GUILTY AS charged, the judge said. Three years on the shelf. Treatment in lieu of incarceration.

"If you fail to meet these obligations, if you are found in association with any known drug dealers or users, if you are found to be positive for alcohol or any other drug as evidenced by urinalysis or breathalyzer, if you pick up any new charge, if you get so much as a parking ticket, you will serve your full sentence with no hope of parole."

He set down the papers. "Do you understand me?"

"I got to go to a program?"

"And you will complete the program."

"I ain't gonna go back to prison?"

"Not if you follow the rules of your probation."

Maggie cut her eye toward her lawyer. Ain't he the smug one, she thought.

The judge went on. "But if you fail to comply with these provisions, if you miss so much as a single meeting with your probation officer or with any counselor, therapist, or case manager recommended for you by your probation officer, I will see to it that you serve every minute of this suspended incarceration. Moreover, if you are caught so much as looking in the direction of a known user or seller of drugs, you will serve out the sentence that I have decided, this one time and against my better judgment, to suspend. Do you understand me?"

Maggie understood; she nodded her head to let him know she understood.

"For the record, Maggie, do you understand what I just told you?"

"Yes." She glanced toward Cooper. He nodded. "Yes, your honor," she said. "I do."

"So if I ever see you in this courtroom again during those three years or after, I will personally and promptly see to it that they put you *under* the jail."

❖ ❖ ❖

"YOU'D OF thought somebody would have been there for me," she told her husband over the phone. "But there wasn't a soul in that room there to back me up. There was Cooper, but he was paid to be there, you know what I mean? It's not the same. And he's just buddying up with those courthouse cronies and cutting deals instead of getting me off, cause, I know I done a lot of things in my time, but this is one time I didn't do what they got me accused of. And I still got convicted. And now I'm on probation, they won't let me visit you in the jail no more. I'm just lucky they let me make this phone call. And they're talking about sending me to some treatment center in a whole nother county, so I might as well be locked up."

"But, Maggie, it's . . ."

"And I can't believe that motherfucking whore boldface lied on the stand like that. On the stand! Perjured her ass bigger than life. I mean, don't they put people in jail for lying on the stand?"

"You ever done anything and not got caught?"

Maggie paused. She knew where this was going to go.

"I don't want to sound mean, but if you'd got what you deserved, you'd be wearing the orange jump suit and I'd be the one sitting on the porch."

"But the bitch lied."

"And you never lied?"

"I never lied on the stand."

"Maggie . . ."

"I always owned up to my shit."

"Maggie!" he said it sharp this time. "You know better and I know better and whoever's tapping this phone will know better if I have to spell it out."

She was quiet for a moment. "No," she said. "You don't need to spell it out."

A buzzer went off somewhere on her husband's end of the line. "I got to go now, Maggie. We'll talk tomorrow."

For a moment, Maggie couldn't speak.

"Maggie?"

"They'll still let you take my call?"

"They'll let us talk. Me and Irby go way back."

Maggie thought she should say something, but she could not find words.

"Do you hear me, Maggie? It's lights out. They're taking us back to the pod."

Maggie found her voice and said goodnight. She set the phone back on its cradle but she did not let it go. She sat and held onto the handset for several minutes before she finally reached around for her cigarettes. She tapped one out and lit it. She turned on the radio, just for the noise of it, and sat smoking with full attention. She smoked the cigarette down to the filter, stubbed it out fiercely, and reached for the phone again.

This time, she called her mother and asked to talk to the kids.

And yes, she knew it was a school night and yes, she knew it was late but no her mother would not wake them at such an hour and why did she call anyway at such an hour; what was she thinking? And yes, her mother knew she had gone to court but she had other things to do. And Maggie understood that but she swore she didn't do it and now she had to go to treatment and no, she didn't see how that could be a good thing when she didn't even do it. And no, you don't understand you never did understand. You just left me to fend for myself and now you won't even let a mother talk to her children. I don't care what hour it is and no, I'm not high but I might as well be for all the respect I get and all the good it does me to try and do right, now don't hang up no don't.

But the line went dead on her mother's end.

This time, Maggie threw the phone down hard; it bounced off the cradle and clattered onto the floor.

❖ ❖ ❖

IT WOULDN'T be so bad, Maggie thought, it if wasn't for the boys across the road up on Pillhead Hill.

From early in the morning and late into the night, cars ran up Maggie's road from the south and down her road from the north. One by one, the tires of the cars wrestled with the turn, rattled the plank floor of the bridge over the creek, and barked up the gravel lane to the top of the hill.

All Maggie had to do was walk across the road and climb the hill and the boys at the top of the hill would take care of her. She had been up that hill and she knew that whatever she wanted—speed, Oxys, weed—the boys on the hill would have it. And if she had no money, they would front her, as any good neighbor would do.

But she could not relieve herself of the glare of the judge. All day long and late into the night, she felt the galvanized eye of the judge pierce her and fix her in place like a butterfly on a pin.

❖ ❖ ❖

"SO, MAGGIE," the probation officer said. "We meet again."
Her PO was a black-headed, black-bearded bear of a man whose elbows occupied most of a small wooden desk. He folded his big hands, hunched his shoulders, and loomed across the desk.

"We're right back where we started."

Maggie had been waiting in the hall outside his office for the better part of an hour; she was ready for a cigarette. "How long will this take?"

"How much time do you have?"

"Not much. I got to be somewhere."

"Well, Maggie. Right now, I think you're right where you need to be."

Maggie was not convinced of that, but she stayed in her seat. "All right," she said. "What do we have to do?"

There were papers to sign. Rules to review. "It's real simple," he said. "If you stay away from the alcohol and drugs, pay me a visit once a week, and stay out of trouble, then you get to stay out of jail."

"So why do I have to go to treatment?"

"Maggie, if you didn't need the treatment, you wouldn't need to ask."

"I've been clean for two months or more."

He thumbed through her file until he came to a lab report. "More like a month and half."

"Whatever. I've stayed clean for three and four months before."

"And what happened?"

Maggie looked at her watch, realized she didn't have a watch, then looked around the room for a clock on the wall.

"Exactly. You got high again. You see," he said, "lots of people can stay clean for a good long while if they have something external, like the threat of prison, to keep them on track. But to make it last . . ."

"Okay, so what about . . ."

He cut her off with a quick gesture. "To make it last," he said, "you have to learn to want it."

"And going to treatment is gonna make that happen?"

"If you let it happen."

"What about the known users and sellers part?"

"That too."

"So how am I supposed to stay away from users and sellers when half the county is either using or selling or both and everybody knows who's using and selling and nobody does a thing about it?"

"Do you know how porcupines make love?"

Here's another motherfucker pleased with himself, she thought. She sat as grim as she knew how and glared at him. "You know she lied, don't you?"

"Who lied?"

"That bitch that testified against me."

The PO looked around the room. "Is she in here?"

"Hell no, she ain't here."

"Then I don't see what she's got to do with what we're talking about."

"I wouldn't be here if it wasn't for her."

"Well, remind me to send her a thank you note."

"Thank you note for what?"

"See, you're on a track to be another statistic. But I'm convinced you can make it if you get the right help. She's your ticket to getting the help."

"She's a lying little crack whore is what she is."

"You know you never answered my question."

"What question?"

"How do porcupines make love?"

"What the hell do I know about a porcupine?"

"You know about those sharp quills. You know that if you get too close, you're liable to get stung."

"And . . ."

"So how do porcupines make love?"

"I don't know. Tell me."

"Very carefully."

"So what's your point?"

"Did you ever know a porcupine to hang around with a lying crack whore?"

"Of course not."

"That's one reason I've never had a porcupine in this office. They don't hang around with lying crack whores."

"Can I go now?"

"Be careful, Maggie. Be very careful who you hang out with. And don't go climbing up Pillhead Hill."

❖ ❖ ❖

"SO WHY do they have to pick on me," Maggie wanted to know, "when there's half a dozen meth labs right under their noses?"

"Which they offered you a chance to name some names and break down the charges," her husband said from his end of the phone, "and you wouldn't take it."

"Which is why I'm still alive to tell you about it. And how did you hear that anyway?"

"Walls talk, babe."

"Damn walls never talked to me when I was in the can."

"It's because you never learned to listen."

"I listen to you, don't I?"

Her old man was silent for a moment.

Oh shit, she thought. He's gonna tell me something I don't want to hear.

"Maggie," he said. He may have been set to tell her something she didn't want to hear, but the buzzer sounded from his end of the line.

"It's lights out, Maggie," he said. "I got to go."

❖ ❖ ❖

A FEW days later, an old friend got Maggie a job waiting tables at the Square Deal Grill just opposite the courthouse. Out the front window, if she stood right, she could see the jailhouse and the window where she thought her man might sometimes look out. Edie O'Leary worked the same shift and picked her up in the morning and brought her home in the afternoon. They were nice to let her work, knowing her record and all and knowing she would have to go for treatment as soon as a bed was open.

"You do right, Maggie," the owner said, "we'll stand by you. You do right, you'll always have a job here."

He did not say what would happen if she did not do right. But she intended to do as right as she knew how. She had no intention of sitting under the steel-eyed glare of that judge again. She had no intention of taking that van back to Marysville.

Once or twice a week, the judge came in for lunch or for coffee and pie. Sometimes, he nodded to her. Sometimes, he spoke. Most times, he ignored Maggie altogether. Which was a blessing to Maggie, for she could not look at the metal in his eye lest he pin her in place with a coffee pot in her hand.

Three weeks into the job, with everything going well, that girl who lied put her head in the door. Things were slow after the breakfast run and Maggie had paused to stretch a newspaper over the counter. The only customer was a logger with wood chips in his hair sitting over coffee at the counter three stools down.

The girl paused to speak to someone in the street, started to walk toward the counter, then saw Maggie and stopped as if she had hit a wall.

"You lying bitch," Maggie whispered. I'll kill her, she thought. I'll kill her right here.

The girl backed up. Her face went pale as bone; her eyes went dark. Her right hand searched the pocket of her coat; her left hand reached to find the door handle.

Maggie slapped the paper down. She would have pounced on the girl like a cat on a mole but for the counter in her way. By the time the girl found the door handle, Maggie was out from behind the counter, but Edie had her by the reins of her apron strings.

"I'll kill her," Maggie said. "I'll kill her right there in the street."

"No, you won't," Edie said. "I'll kill you first." She grabbed Maggie by the shoulder, pulled her back two steps, and moved in front to block Maggie from the door.

Maggie side-stepped. Edie stepped with her, then back when Maggie tried again. Satisfied that she had Maggie stopped for now, she stuck a bony finger like a pistol right between Maggie's eyes. "Back up," she said. "Go straight back behind that counter," she said.

"Stay there and read your damn newspaper."

❖ ❖ ❖

AND THEN one day there was Randy the Man.

"Here's your neighbor," Edie said. She touched Maggie at the elbow and pointed to the front booth.

Randy the Man was the chief of the boys on Pillhead Hill. He was tall and built like a bullet. He had eyes gray as lead and long gray hair cinched at the back of his neck. Blue tattoos too dense and obscure to read or interpret ran all up and down his arms and around his neck like the collar of a priest. He walked the square broad step of a wrestler, which they said he had been, though not one of the famous ones, so when he strode into the Square Deal Grill, it was as if he were working his way through the crowd and up to the ring. It was as if he could hear the announcer call out, *Here we have Randy the Man.*

"I can't wait on him," Maggie said.

"It's your table," Edie said.

"You don't understand."

"It's your table."

"You don't fucking understand."

"You told me you didn't ever score from him."

"I don't. I mean, I don't score from anybody now. But I never did. Or I did, but I couldn't deal with the drama. It was Dodge City up there, all them guns and hookers and young girls and I'm like . . ."

"He needs his coffee."

No one knew Randy the Man last summer when he first bought the old Stephens place across the creek and up the hill from Maggie's house. But they all knew him soon enough.

He paid cash up front, they said. And never blinked at the price. He just reached in his pocket and peeled off bills like cabbage leaves.

That got people's attention. But when he started selling OxyContin off the front porch, his name was on every tongue.

Maggie got on the phone to her husband. "It can't last," she said. "There's too many people that know too much."

"Well, then stay away," he said.

"I don't want to be nowhere near that hill when it all goes to hell in a handbasket."

But the months turned around and the raid never came. Who was Randy paying off? Whose pocket was he lining? Or was he just that slick?

Night after night, cars ran down the road from the north or up the road from the south, cars in all states of operation, rumbling, rattling, or humming, to scrawl around the turn onto Randy's lane, rattle the bridge floor, and mount the gravel lane to where Randy waited on the porch, ready to take the driver for that little walk back into the woods.

"I think he's up there committing slow suicide," Maggie told her old man. She had her own connections, so she stayed away, even after Randy told her, right on the courthouse square, "We got you covered," by which she understood that Randy the Man would front her if ever she came up dry.

And many a night, when she couldn't hook up, Maggie had lain in a detoxified fever, burning and nauseous, crazy sick, her shocked cells demanding just a little hit, just a stupid little up-front hit to take this pain away.

She shivered and cursed and hoped to die, but I'm damned, she thought, if I'm gonna go up that hill.

Eventually, sometimes, she did. Terrible things happened, but sometimes she made that climb.

But that was over now. She was through with Pillhead Hill and anyone associated with it.

"What if my PO sees me?"

"You're not setting up housekeeping with him," Edie said.

"But . . ."

"It's business," Edie said. "Take care of your business."

Maggie readied a cup and poured it full. She muttered a curse with as low a mutter as she knew how, but Edie said, "He'll want the whole pot, so you might as well bring it over. And I don't care what kind of bitches you call me."

Maggie took the cup in one hand and the pot in the other and muttered her way to Randy's booth. He let her set the coffee in front of him without taking his eye from the window. He waved away the cream and the sugar she tried to give him.

"You doing all right, Maggie?"

"I'm doing fine," she said. She couldn't look at him for fear of the judge, so she looked out the window as well. "Everything's fine," she mumbled.

"Your old man still over in the jailhouse?"

"Yeah, he's still in there."

"And he's got another couple months?"

That, she thought, and another six days. But she just nodded.

"I'm glad to see you working," Randy said. "I thought you were gone to Marysville for sure."

Maggie wanted to tell him all about the little lying crack whore, and the judge with the galvanized eye, but she thought better of it. "I'm still here," she said.

"And I hear you're clean."

She wanted to ask, Who told you that? Instead, she let him tell her how good a thing that was and how she'll not regret it and how he wished he could quit smoking or for that matter this damn coffee which he drank five or ten pots of every day and it's the first thing in the morning and the last thing at night and he don't hardly get any sleep what with the coffee and those boys that's staying with him but hey, people gotta do what they gotta do, you know? They sure like to party, but me, I like to . . .

Randy seemed to have forgotten what he liked. Without another word, he set down his coffee, stood, slapped a five-dollar bill down on the table, and pushed past Maggie and out the door.

He balanced a moment on the front step of the Square Deal Grill. He gave a hard look to the main door of the courthouse, a brief look, a glance, but hard enough to drive a nail. Then he crossed the sidewalk in his squared-up wrestler's walk, opened the door of his Jeep, hammered another glance toward the courthouse door, settled in behind the wheel, and drove off with his fat tires squealing.

A moment later, as if summoned by Randy's hard eye, Maggie's judge came out the courthouse door. Not the front door, but a little, hardly used, side door. He walked straight across the lawn to where the county reserved a spot for his SUV, got in, and drove off in the same direction as Randy the Man.

Maggie stared down the street until both cars took the bend in the road and disappeared. Then she took the pot back to the coffee maker.

"You're not gonna believe this," she said.

"I never do," said Edie.

"No, really," Maggie said. "I just saw the judge that sentenced me take off after Randy the Man."

"And?"

"Why would that judge want to see Randy the Man?"

"He's a judge. He can see anybody he wants."

"Well, what's he gonna do with Randy the Man?"

"He's a judge. He can do what he wants."

"But what if he's buying drugs?"

"He's a judge."

"But don't he have to follow the law like the rest of us?"

"How many judges did you know up in Marysville?"

"Not a one."

"There's my point."

"What point?"

"He's a judge. He's got the law in his hip pocket."

"But that ain't right."

"Maggie, what do you know about right? You been wrong since you first drew breath and now you want to talk about right?"

Why, Maggie wondered, is everybody so dedicated to setting me straight?

"You don't know any more than a bird about what that judge is up to. You don't even know for sure he was following Randy."

"I seen him."

"You just happened to see him get in a car right after Randy the Man got in a car and you just happened to see him drive for a few blocks that just happened to be in the same direction as Randy the Man. And you think you can make a case from that?"

I saw what I saw, thought Maggie. I saw what I saw.

❖ ❖ ❖

ONE AFTER another, day and night, the cars came down Maggie's road from the north and up her road from the south. They worked through the turn, shook the bridge floor, scratched their way up the hill and, minutes later, rolled back down. Sometimes, a bright, new SUV scrambled up the hill and an old beater rolled back down and Maggie knew that someone had gotten the bad end of a deal and their car would end up in the row of cars parked behind the house. And one day she thought she knew the SUV that went up the hill and thought she saw her judge driving the beater that came back.

This ain't right, she thought. But she said nothing at the Grill and nothing on the phone to her old man.

And the boys on Pillhead Hill continued night and day. Sometimes, when the wind was right, Maggie heard snatches of music way up into the night, or high-pitched women's laughter, or the gunning of a motorcycle that set the dogs to barking all up and down the road.

As the cars came from north and south, each one bore a bank account, a week's pay, or fifty dollars from selling off the piano someone's grandmother left them. They carried the college tuition, the Christmas toys for the kids, the house payment, the support payment, the car payment that was overdue. They carried the egg money or tobacco money or money earned giving blowjobs to truckers. Entire houses went up the hill, along with farms and small businesses, reputations, and self-respect. Years went uphill, bundled like cordwood, stacked for sale, ready to burn.

It's a terrible thing that happens up there on that hill, Maggie thought. But she longed for the terrible thing. Each frailed and fouled nerve was alert to the chance. Each addled neuron ached to be filled with that ecstasy and disaster.

She only wanted a reason.

❖ ❖ ❖

SHE WAS in the habit of calling Gary the last thing at night before he had lights out and before she had to try to sleep before work. But this time when she called, it wasn't Irby, the usual second-shift jailer.

"Who's this?" she asked.

"Officer Weatherstone."

"Timmy?"

"Who's this?"

"Timmy, let me talk to Gary real quick before it's lights out."

"Can't do it, Maggie."

"Why not? I call every night."

"I got orders, Maggie."

He had orders. She argued, but Timmy Weatherstone had orders, in writing, in plain sight, and he didn't care what Irby did on his shift and he wasn't going to let her talk to him like that and how did she get this number anyway? She cursed him seven times blue and reminded him what a snake he had for a mother before he hung up on her with a curse of his own and she thought, Now I've gone and done it. She was gospel sure she was headed off to Marysville on the next bus north.

So why not?

❖ ❖ ❖

THIS IS just like death, Maggie thought. She was warm; she was at peace; she was free of pain. Everything was still. She was swaddled in light.

She tested her limbs and found that her arms and legs were heavy as timber.

This is what death is like, she thought. This might be death itself.

But death would not perch an IV bottle over her like a plastic buzzard. Death would not run a tube down into her arm and death would not post a monitor with red blinking lights by her bedside. She propped herself up and widened her gaze. Death, she knew, was not a hospital room and death would not leave so bearish a man asleep in a chair nearby.

She thought she knew him, but she did not know the big yellow teeth exposed by the man's slack jaw. Perhaps he sensed that someone was staring at him, for he caught himself mid-snore, pulled his lips down over the teeth, and looked around. When he saw it was Maggie, he brightened.

"So you're back among the living," he said.

"What're you doing here?"

"I've been taking a little power nap," he said. "The real question is, what are you doing here?"

Maggie looked around and shrugged. "I don't even know how I got here," she said.

"You know you just about took the big nap," he said.

She shrugged, as if to say she would not have minded. "So I reckon I'll be going back to prison."

"Maggie," he said. "If you can't be careful you might as well be lucky. And you're a lucky woman. You're lucky to be alive and you're lucky enough to time your overdose for a Friday night just before a treatment bed came open."

"So what does that mean?"

"It means that if I can get you out of here and into that treatment bed before court opens on Monday, you don't go back to prison."

"What day is it now?"

"It's Sunday evening, we've got to be rolling."

Within an hour, Maggie was pronounced fit to leave. A nurse untethered her from the IV and the monitor, stood her up on her shaky feet, helped her dress, and rolled her in a wheelchair to the parking lot where her PO waited in his car.

It was dark and snow had begun to fall as they pulled out of the lot.

"Can I go home first?"

"We're not taking any chances." He took one big paw off the steering wheel and pointed to the backseat with his thumb. "Your girlfriend from the Grill packed a duffel for you. No need to risk starting this whole thing over."

Maggie fretted in her seat. "The meds is starting to wear off," she said. "I'm gonna start geeking soon."

"We'll get you there soon enough. And they'll give you whatever you need."

Maggie was not convinced, but there was nothing she could do about it. The treatment people, she knew, would just tell her to tough it out. She did not feel tough at all, but she would have to tough it out. She slumped in her seat and watched the lights of the houses roll by. Here and there, she caught a glimpse into a kitchen or a living room—a couple at table or the flicker of a television—and felt lonely and out of sorts.

What a mess my life has been, she thought.

They left town and the fields began to open up around them. The lights were fewer than before. They hit the highway and the car began to pick up speed. Her PO, who had been silent and wary as they drove through town, began to talk about this and that and Maggie supposed that she should listen. But mile after mile, she continued to watch the lights tick by, the near lights and the lights far out on the hills, lights that in their distance might as well have been stars.

The Girl Who Spoke Foreign

THAT GIRL was talking in her sleep again.

Maggie Boylan sat up in her bed and listened. Everything else was quiet. Outside her window, snow fell on silent snow. The third shift monitors were dozing at their stations. Everyone else was sound asleep. Everything else was perfectly still. There was only this muttering girl with her moans and curses.

Oh fuck, Maggie thought, not again.

The way she talked was some kind of foreign, so that *Please* came out as *Pliz!* And *Pliz no!* So, over and over, it was *Pliz!* And *Pliz!* And *No!* And then a long string of perfectly crafted curses. Then the curses trailed off and the girl moaned and muttered and twitched and gasped and Maggie knew that, for the second night running, she could have no hope of sleeping.

The girl was just a young girl, barely old enough to be in this place. But she carried such a burden of cursing and grief. She was a tiny little thing, skinny as a weasel and just as loopy. But she bellowed out her curses like a bull in rut, curses not even Maggie would curse, curses made up of words Maggie could not even understand but which she knew to be curses by the vehemence of them and by the way it broke her heart to hear them.

The girl twitched and gasped so that Maggie couldn't bear it, and she stood, threw her jacket over her shoulders, and stared as the girl mumbled and muttered and sighed and pulled the blankets up around her neck.

All day long, she don't have two words to say, Maggie thought. Then she goes to sleep and she can't shut up. Maggie had tried last night to sleep on one of the couches in the group room, but the third shift people had run her back to her room. She had begged to be switched to another room, but they turned her down. She had tried stuffing her ears with tissue, but the tissues fell out. So she was stuck with all this muttering and cursing that made it impossible to sleep.

It's that powerless shit, Maggie thought. I'm powerless. And powerless means you're fucked.

It was bad enough that she was stuck in here with all these mental cases—Maggie knew she had a little problem with OxyContin, but she wasn't mental—but then she had to put up with this little girl with the big barrel of a voice.

Tomorrow, when Maggie fell asleep again in group, that skinny little vixen who ran it would tell her again she was being resistant.

But she wasn't resistant. She sat when she was supposed to sit and she stood when she was supposed to stand and she read what they told her to read and she wrote what they told her to write and she joined hands in the circle and mumbled the prayer along with the rest.

Resistant! she thought. If she wants to see resistant, I can resist my ass right out the door and up the road.

But she knew what was up the road. The judge had laid it out for her.

❖ ❖ ❖

THE GIRL fell silent for a moment, but Maggie knew better than to hope. And sure enough, in seconds, it was *Pliz!* And *No!* And a new string of curses. *Pliz!* and *Pliz no!* she called over and over and it was clear that, in whatever desperate dream she was in, the girl was pleading. She settled down to muttering again and Maggie thought, if the girl would just keep it at that level, I might be able to sleep through it after all. But right in the middle of the muttering, the girl sat bolt upright. "*No!*" she shouted. "*Pliz no!*"

They say you shouldn't wake them, Maggie remembered, though she couldn't see what harm it would do. The girl didn't shout again and, after several minutes, the wild, tormented dream seemed to have left her. But the girl suddenly sucked in air as if she had been punched. She held her breath for several long seconds, then released as if she had just surrendered. Maggie pulled her chair over to the girl's bed and sat where she could watch more closely. Over and over the girl sucked in air, held it, and released it. But at least for now, she was done with the shouts and the curses.

Quiet as a mouse in the daytime, Maggie thought. But she's the handbells of hell at night.

To look at her in the daytime, who would ever know? When first she saw her, Maggie thought the girl was part of the staff, she looked so serene and untroubled. She was so blond and perfect— movie star blond and movie star perfect—that the men on the unit and even the counselors and even the doctor on his stroll— each did that little jiggle of the head where they wanted to turn and follow her around the room, but didn't want to show it.

Quiet as a mouse, with dark, wide eyes like those of a mouse caught in a trap. To Maggie, she seemed a timid, useless mouse of a thing. But that did not stop the men from turning her way. The girl endured the eyes, when she lifted her own to see them, with an unreadable look that seemed alternately sly and despairing.

The girl was blond in the daylight, but in the moonlight from the window her hair looked white as lamb's wool, her face pale, her brow flexed tight as corduroy. Gradually, the girl's breathing leveled, her brow relaxed; she began to breathe soft and natural as a baby.

Such a baby, Maggie thought. I wish the fuck she would let me sleep, but she's such a poor fucked-up baby.

And through the small hours, until she finally fell asleep in her chair, Maggie watched over the white-haired girl as over a child.

❖ ❖ ❖

SOMETIME IN the middle of the night, a man and a woman from the third shift stood on either side of her and wanted to know, "Are you all right?"

"I was fine till you woke me up," Maggie muttered. She cursed them both with no real enthusiasm—she knew she had been beaten on that count—and they guided her or lifted her— she couldn't remember which—from the chair to the bed.

Finally, the morning light and the chatter of the morning birds woke her. Maggie sat up and looked around.

The girl was gone. Her bed was made up neat as if it had been an envelope licked and sealed. And all her little items, her books, her makeup, her lotion bottles, and whatnot, were tidied on the dresser top like soldiers in formation.

The loudspeaker went off and Maggie guessed it was the breakfast call. But that was only a guess. There was no real way a body could tell what fell from those wheezy, asthmatic speakers. She knew they said breakfast or lunch because everyone else started for the cafeteria. She knew it announced group because they all headed for the group room. But anything else might as well have been in French or even in the girl's incomprehensible language.

Maggie pulled herself up and looked out the window. The birds had gathered at a feeder in the yard below. Beyond the yard, a wire fence bordered on a cornfield. Snow lay thick in the furrows; broken, blackened cornstalks rose up among the snow like scratches on a page. A rooster crowed in the distance. It was a dim winter dawn, gray as gunmetal. Beyond the cornfield, another field, and beyond that, a house or two with the wood smoke rising from the chimneys. Beyond that, the morning mist obscured her view.

The loudspeaker barked again. I got to go, Maggie thought, I'll be late and they'll be writing me up.

❖ ❖ ❖

IT WAS breakfast after all. Maggie was late and the kitchen staff were happy to tell her so. But they didn't write her up, so she kept

her curses under her breath, gulped down her breakfast, and
headed off to group.

In group, Maggie sat silent for as long as she could. The
little vixen was not happy about it and she said so.

"You mean, you've got nothing at all to say?"

Maggie shrugged.

Her little, blond roommate didn't have anything to say
either. Even less, for she would not even talk outside of group.
In fact, Maggie had yet to hear her say a waking word. But the
vixen said nothing to the girl. She was just picking on Maggie
and it was wrong and Maggie would have told her so, but she
knew better. She thought, They're just waiting for me to say
something so they'll have an excuse to kick me out.

"Nothing at all?"

Say something and get kicked out for it. Say nothing and get
kicked out for it—it was that powerless shit again.

"I seem to recall you had a lot to say when they dropped you
off and you had a lot to say when they checked you in and you
had a lot to say when they caught you smoking in the back hall,
but you can't find anything to say now?"

"I'll say this . . ." Maggie spoke the first thought that came to
mind and hoped that might get the vixen off her back. "I'll tell
you this," she said. "I never did trust nobody with a clipboard."

Which was a mistake. The vixen didn't seem bothered in
the least that Maggie didn't trust her. She wanted to know why
and who did she know with a clipboard in the past and what did
a clipboard represent to her and Maggie thought, What the fuck
have I got myself into now?

From there on, it was a tangle. So far as she could recall,
Maggie had never in her life had a thought about a person with
a clipboard. But she couldn't unsay it now she had said it. And
in moments, she was in a briar patch of invented insults and
injuries. It was bankers evicting and auctioneers selling off all
the family treasure and teachers swatting and preachers who
were hypocrites and a store clerk who tried to feel her up when
she was just thirteen.

It wore her out, after so little sleep, to invent so many lies at once and, before ten minutes were out, Maggie felt like her head would split. She had never had trouble coming up with lies before, but the vixen was relentless. She stuck her little fox of a nose into every little nook of every lie she told.

"So," the vixen said. "You don't trust me because I carry a clipboard and you've had all these negative experiences with people who carry clipboards."

Maggie nodded. There wasn't a word of truth to it, but she nodded.

"So maybe this will help." The vixen took her notes from under the clip, gripped the clipboard by one corner, and flung it like a Frisbee. It banked off the wall and fell into the trashcan.

Maggie thought, This girl's a freak.

"Now, I don't have a clipboard. So tell me something."

"Tell you what?"

"Tell me what's the real problem."

"I already told you."

"Because I don't believe a bit of this clipboard bullshit."

"I thought you wasn't supposed to cuss."

"I'm not supposed to throw away a perfectly good clipboard either. But let's talk about you."

The blond girl's mousetrap eyes moved from one to another.

"You ain't talking to her like that," Maggie said. "She ain't said a word in two days and you ain't picking on her."

"Because right now we're focusing on you."

"You can focus on my ass."

"We might do that later. Right now, we're focused on your ability to tell the truth."

The blond girl pulled her feet up on her chair, tucked her knees under her chin, and stared at the floor. Maggie was sorry she had tried to drag the girl into it, sorry she had spoken at all. She suddenly grew desperately tired. Her arms were heavy as bricks. "My God," she muttered. "I want to get out of here so fucking bad."

"Because you feel you're being picked on."

Maggie looked hard at the vixen to see if she could catch any hint of mockery in her face and decided she did not like her either way. "No," she said. "Because this whole place sucks, including you, you little four-eyed bitch."

"Thank you."

"Thank you for what?" Maggie was certain she was fucked for sure now.

"Thank you for saying something real."

"If real is what you're looking for, then fuck you again."

"Because everything you've said before has been a lie."

"So fuck you ten times more."

"And now we get to see the real you."

"And the real me says fuck you till you're cross-eyed."

"Thank you for sharing," the vixen said. "I think we've made some progress."

Maggie would have told her to stick some progress up her skinny ass. But the loudspeaker announced something in asthmatic French and everyone stood for the end of group.

Maggie stood with the rest and held hands with the rest and mumbled the prayer along with the rest, but she swayed with exhaustion and her mind was muddled and confused and she silently cursed the vixen and the blond girl for it.

❖ ❖ ❖

AT LUNCH, she tried to call her husband. Sometimes the jailer would let him talk. But not today—the prick—and she cursed him seven times sideways until he hung up and she thought, now he'll take it out on Gary, which was one more worry to hang around her head.

By midafternoon, Maggie was delirious from lack of sleep. The coffee was weak-ass decaf and they wouldn't let her take a nap. They piss-tested her before supper and Maggie was sure they thought she was high on Oxys again.

If only she was. If only she could have just one sweet little Oxy. Just one would lift her out of this insanity, if only for a little while. If she could, she would, if she could without getting caught. But she was not about to face that judge again.

So she struggled through the rest of her groups and doodled through the art therapy and dozed over her evening meal and tried to follow the story of the AA speaker. She sat when she was supposed to sit and she stood when she was supposed to stand. She read what she was supposed to read and mumbled through the prayers like the rest. For there was no way she would let herself get kicked out of the program and face all that prison time. One day at a time, she thought. One fucking day at a time.

But please, God, not such another day as this.

❖ ❖ ❖

AT BREAK, Maggie went back to her room for a cigarette and her jacket. And there was the girl. She was kneeling on Maggie's bed and looking out the window.

"What's up, babe?"

Startled, the girl turned. She got up from the bed and crossed the room to her own.

"It's okay, honey. You want to look out the window, look out."

The girl stared out of her mousetrap eyes, but said nothing.

"It's okay," Maggie said. "Just look." Maggie knelt on the bed beside her and looked to see what the girl might have seen. "I don't see nothing," she said. "Nothing but snow, but you're welcome to look."

The girl still said nothing, but she crossed the room and joined Maggie at the window.

"Like I say, there ain't nothing out there but . . ."

The girl touched Maggie on the shoulder and put a finger to her lips. She looked out the window and seemed to search each corner, each cap of snow on each fence post. She finished her search, then backed off the bed, and turned to go.

"I wish I knew what you was looking for."

"I watch for those men."

I'll be damned, Maggie thought. She can talk. Her accent was still some sort of foreign. Maggie could not tell what kind of foreign it was, but it was surely not Ohio.

"What men?"

The girl stared at Maggie for a long time before she answered. "I will tell you," she said. "But not now."

"But who . . . ?"

"The men. If they come for me, I will kill myself."

"But . . ."

"I am dead woman either way."

"Who . . ."

She raised her hand to cut off Maggie's question. "*Pliz*," she said. "Don't tell no one."

The loudspeaker coughed out a call to evening meal. The girl touched her finger to her lips again and slipped out of the room.

❖ ❖ ❖

MAGGIE TOLD no one. It was not her nature to tell. The girl resumed her silence through the evening meal, chores, and evening group. She was silent through the AA speakers. She did not so much as look Maggie's way.

Finally, after evening meeting, they were alone in their room.

The girl was in her nightgown and stood in her bare feet near the door. She was ready to switch off the light when Maggie asked, "Why do you talk all night long in your sleep but you won't say a word all day?" Maggie did not expect an answer, but she asked anyway.

The mousetrap eyes grew even wider. "*Whot* did I say?"

"You said a lot, babe."

"*Whot* did I say?"

"You said, 'no' and 'please' over and over, but the rest all sounded foreign."

"Did I say anyone's name?"

"It all sounded foreign to me."

"A name, did I say anyone's name?"

"How would I know a name in foreign?"

The girl sank down into her bed. She looked across the room to the window and shook her head. "I am dead woman," she said to the window.

"You don't look dead to me. And you sure don't sound dead at night."

The girl shook her head. "Tomorrow, next day—who knows?—they come for me." Then she rolled over in her bed and faced the wall and pulled the blanket up to her ears.

In minutes, she was asleep. Maggie could tell because she started again to gasp, hold her breath, and release. But in a few minutes more, she was breathing soft as a kitten.

If the girl shouted in the night again, Maggie did not know it, for she was drowned in her own sleep and her dreams were burdened with curses.

❖ ❖ ❖

MAGGIE WOKE in the morning, miserable and alert.

The girl was already up, tidying her bed, folding down the corners neat as that envelope.

"How are you this morning, Dead Woman?"

"Is not a joke," the girl said. She pulled her sheets tight with a snap, then raised herself to look at Maggie with her unreadable eyes.

"Is not a joke," she said. "Pliz do not laugh." She narrowed her eyes. "Do not laugh," she said.

❖ ❖ ❖

HER NAME was Marina. And she came from some unpronounceable country where they convince the young girls they're headed to America for jobs as nurses or secretaries and they trap them into prostitution. They rape them and they pump them full of drugs and they put them to work as prostitutes.

"Slave," she said. "I was slave. Even now I am not free, but there I was slave."

Even when the police raided the place where they worked her, she had not been freed. The men got away; the police charged her with prostitution and a judge sent her to this place.

"The men ran. But they will be back to find me."

"You sure? You don't think they've maybe learned their lesson?"

"You do not know them. They learn no lessons. They want me back. I tried to run. But they brought me back."

Maggie's heart ached for the girl. "I don't know what to say, babe."

"Say nothing. You can say nothing to a dead woman."

❖ ❖ ❖

THE NEXT morning, the girl pointed out the window. "Look," she said. She said it foreign, like *Luke*. "Luke," she pointed.

Maggie looked with her. "I don't see nothing," she said.

"Luke, there," she said. "By the fence."

Maggie saw only the fence line and the snow and the black stalks of corn.

"Footprints," she said. She said it like *boot prints*.

"It's probably a farmer," Maggie said. "Checking his fence line."

"Is no farmer."

"Where do you see these prints?"

"There," she pointed. "Luke," she said. "The footprints stop there. Across from these window. They stop there. They stand there. And they watch."

Maggie looked, but she could not see what the girl saw in the snow. She saw the yard and the birdseed frittered over the snow. She saw the fence and the field beyond the fence. "I still think it's just a farmer."

"Is the farmer of souls."

"How is the farmer of souls gonna find you here?"

"They know."

"And how they gonna get you out of here?"

"I dunno. I just want to die." She balled up her fists, bowed her head, and began to pound her temples. "I just want to go somewhere and die."

"Honey, don't say that."

"What can I say? I have no way to live."

"You can live, babe. I've lived through some shit, you can too."

The girl looked at Maggie with her unreadable look that may have been sly or it may have been despairing. "I have to run," she said.

"Where you gonna go?"

"I dunno. I dunno. But if I stay here I am dead woman." She began to grab the ranked soldiers at the top of her dresser and throw them into a backpack.

"Tell the staff. They won't let them past the desk."

She laughed a dead woman's laugh. "Front desk will not stop them."

"Well, the front desk will sure enough try to stop you if you try to leave."

"I go out back."

"And set off the alarm. Think about it."

The girl set down the backpack and sank onto her bed. "I am dead woman."

"Not yet. Let's think."

"I cannot think."

"A plan," Maggie said. "What you need is a plan."

The girl brooded while Maggie thought.

"I don't reckon it would help to call the sheriff."

The girl smirked. "The police tell them go away, they go away. But they come back. I tell you I am dead woman."

Maggie looked at the little plastic sandals the girl was wearing. "You got better shoes than that?"

"These are the shoes they give a dead woman."

"You're sure enough dead if you try to walk through the snow in those things." Her jacket was even worse, a little thin thing made for style but no good for keeping a body warm.

They agreed that the girl would take Maggie's coat and shoes. It was a good coat—her old man's denim coat with a quilted lining. And they were good shoes—high-top work shoes. Maggie could pretend the girl stole them. Maggie could create a diversion and the girl would slip out of a first-floor window and walk across the hills to the next little town where there was a homeless shelter. It had started to snow again. That

would make it harder going, but it would cover up her tracks.
From there, who knew? The girl would have to figure it out
from there.

It worked. Maggie picked an argument with the second shift
staff. She got rowdy enough to get everyone's attention, settled
it just short of getting herself written up, then a little later,
raised a second ruckus over the little blond bitch who stole her
shoes and coat.

❖   ❖   ❖

MAGGIE THOUGHT that, without the girl's nightmare racket,
she would sleep easy. Instead, she fretted, tossed, and worried
about the girl. She could not help thinking about what might
happen. Would they track her down? Would she freeze to death
out there in the snow?

Finally, she thought, Hell with this. I need a smoke. She
tossed back the covers, got out of bed, and got a lighter and a
cigarette. The monitor at the desk was looking at bikini models
in a magazine and never looked up when she asked. He pointed
toward the door and nodded.

The prissy shoes the girl had left behind hurt her feet and
they were little slim things so that the cold of the snow went right
up through the soles. I need to make this quick, she thought. She
pulled the girl's thin jacket close around her and lit up. The smoke
felt good, the last thing she had to feel good about.

She shivered through her cigarette. She smoked it down to
the filter tip and made ready to flip it over the fence and into
the field. She launched it and watched the arc of it over the
barbwire fence to where it died in the snow with a hiss.

She knocked on the door to get back in and waited for the
monitor. And waited. And muttered and cursed the cold and
the silly shoes the girl had left her and the habit of cigarette
smoking and the entire race of monitors.

A car came down the road. She heard the engine growl out
of the curve and she saw the headlights cross the hedges. Then
as it passed, she saw the blood-red taillights brighten as it pulled

to a stop about a hundred yards down the cornfield and far from the lights of the farmhouses.

The monitor finally came padding down the hall and opened the door. "Come on in, Maggie," he said.

"Hold on," she said.

"It's too damn cold to hold on."

"Hold on. Just a minute."

There were voices now.

"What are you doing out here?"

"I'm looking at this car."

"It's too damn cold to look at a car."

"Hold on." Maggie strained to hear the voices. "Just a minute," she said.

"Maggie, I got to do rounds."

"Do your rounds," she said. "Come back for me later."

The monitor let the door fall shut, then muttered down the hall and cursed his way around the corner. Out in the snow, the voices, half-hushed and argumentative, rose and fell and rose and fell and Maggie could not make out a word of it from the distance and from the muffling of the snow. But she could make out the voice of a woman from out in the field and the voice of a man from the car and she could hear the voices coming closer together.

Oh my God, she thought. Oh, please Jesus, no.

The voices argued closer until the woman came into the range of the headlights and Maggie could see that the woman was small, that she wore an oversized, dark coat, and that, in the headlights of the car, her hair looked white as the snow around her.

Please Jesus, no, Maggie thought again.

The woman sputtered and cursed as the man helped her over the barbwire fence and they got into the car and left.

Please God, no, Maggie prayed. Over and over, she shivered and cursed and prayed.

The car was long gone when the monitor came off his rounds. "Come on, Maggie," he said. "You'll catch your death out here."

Maggie shivered once more and stared toward the road.

"Maggie," the monitor called. When she turned to go in, her face was damp with tears and snot and snow.

Acceptance Is the Answer

MAGGIE BOYLAN got out of treatment at nine in the morning. The third shift monitor was going her way, so he stuck around for the coin ceremony and the speeches and the hugs, and then he took her up to town and dropped her off on the courthouse square. She took a look around, took a deep breath of the open air, and walked straight up to the jailhouse door.

She walked straight back out when they told her that her husband was gone. "We turned him loose a week ago," said Tim Weatherstone.

She had amends to make to Tim Weatherstone. She had amends to make to nearly every deputy on the force. And she was ready. But when she heard that Gary had been released, it took her by surprise. Why didn't he call? Why didn't he visit? She blazed a path of curses straight out the door and onto the courthouse lawn. Why hadn't he come to see her like she had come to see him?

After she had cursed Tim Weatherstone and her husband and her luck from the lawn of the courthouse, she calmed down and thought. She had learned in treatment not to ask so many useless questions; she had learned not to make assumptions. Hell, she thought, Gary's got no license and he's got no car. And nobody's paid the phone bill for three months.

Edie O'Leary let her call from the Square Deal Grill and, sure enough, a recording told her that the phone was disconnected.

So she walked to the edge of town and stood on the highway with her thumb out. It was nine miles and a side road to home. It was early spring. The dogwoods were out but not yet the redbuds. There was still some bite in the wind. There were still patches of snowmelt in the shady places along the fence lines and in the ditches. Some girl in treatment had stolen her jacket and her good shoes and left her with these girly thin things that pinched her toes and a little thin jacket that wouldn't hold out the wind. Someone else had left behind a backpack like what a schoolgirl might carry and she had packed it with her Big Book, her clothes, her toothbrush, and other odds and ends. She shivered and stamped, but she was happy to be out on her own and anxious to see Gary again.

It was only a few minutes before a pickup truck pulled over and she thought maybe her luck had begun to turn. It was a big-shouldered, diesel-motored F-350 lugging a stock trailer. She ran down to catch up and the driver opened the door to let her in.

But when she saw who the driver was, she thought, Oh no, this is trouble. It was Joey Ratliff, a boy she knew for all the wrong reasons.

"What's cracking, Maggie?"

"Not much," she said. She hesitated before she climbed up into the cab. He's gonna want me to get him some dope again, she thought. Two hours out of treatment, and I'm already in a risky situation.

"Come on, Maggie," Joey said. "These girls in the trailer aren't too happy with me." The cattle in the trailer were miserable. They moaned and bawled piteously. They pressed their snouts against the slats in the trailer and looked out at Maggie with dark, wet eyes.

"Come on in, and get yourself out of the cold," the boy said.

This won't look good to the judge, Maggie thought. Miller had told her, no contact with known users or dealers or else she would serve the prison time he had suspended. But Miller was not out here standing in the wind with her in a little thin jacket and these little, thin, girly shoes. So she mounted the step into the cab.

Joey Ratliff put the truck into gear and they pulled off with a great rattle of pistons and a mantle of diesel smoke behind them. The boy had the heater cranked up good and warm. The seats were leather and the console was lit up like a small city. Maggie was glad for the warmth, but she tried to keep her head low so no one could see her.

"So what's new, Maggie?"

"Not much at all," she told the boy. "I been away."

"I heard," the boy said. "And you just now got out."

"So you heard that too?"

"Word gets around," he said.

"I reckon so."

"You can't cuss out half the sheriff's department on the courthouse square without people knowing Maggie Boylan's back in town."

"Well, damn." She fell silent and wanted to think. But it was hard to think with the poor cattle bawling in the trailer. The boy was none too steady on the road and the trailer lurched back and forth across the lanes. The cattle bawled and moaned with every lurch.

"Hell," he said. "It ain't nothing."

It was something to Maggie. It could be three years in prison if the judge heard. And how would Miller not hear if this boy had heard already?

"Just party hearty and forget about it."

"I can't, Joey." Maggie surprised herself by finding the words so easily. "My party-er's broke."

Joey Ratliff pondered this a moment. "That's rough," he said. "I reckon you're just gonna have to accept it. Acceptance," he said, "is the answer to all my problems."

Joey Ratliff had done his time in treatment too.

They were on a downhill curve and the boy had to snatch the wheel hard to the left to keep out of the ditch then to the right to get out of the path of an oncoming car. The trailer behind them rattled over the shoulder gravel and swung into the opposite lane and nearly clipped the car.

Maggie had to grip the door handle to stay in her seat. The cattle, the poor cattle, bawled the louder.

"Damn," Maggie shouted. "You're gonna kill us all."

"It's all right."

She saw, now, that the boy's eyes had an OxyContin glaze on them. His words had an OxyContin loop to them. He drove like someone in an OxyContin haze.

"Joey, you sure you need to be driving?"

"I'm all right," he said. "Acceptance."

I'm about to accept getting run into one of these telephone poles, Maggie thought. She kept her grip on the door handle and watched the road. Joey wasn't driving fast, but he was nearly always half a beat behind each dip or swerve. Neither spoke for an uncomfortable minute or two. Finally, to make talk, Maggie said, "Your daddy's got a nice truck."

The boy was the son of a county commissioner and things had looked good for him all through high school. College offers, scholarships, all that. But after graduation, he had got caught up in OxyContin, so all his luck and privilege came to nothing. She was not surprised when he asked, "So, Maggie. Can you help me get hold of some Oxy?"

"Can't do it, Joey."

"How about some Vicodin? Percocets?"

"Can't do it."

"Sure you can."

"Does the word *prison* mean anything to you? I got three years setting on the shelf. I'm out of that game altogether."

"Maggie, you know I'm cool."

A truck, passing, barely missed the corner of the stock trailer. "You ain't looking any too cool right now, I'd say."

"Well, if you won't get me some yourself, can you hook me up with those boys on the hill?"

"What boys on what hill?"

"Across the road from your house. Those boys from the city at the old Stephens place. Pillhead Hill."

"Why would I want to do that?"

"You could help a fella out."

"Joey, you're gonna have to help yourself out on this one."

"Come on, Maggie. They don't know me."

"Just ride on up there and get to know them."

"Maggie, you know I can't just do that."

"I don't know what you can and can't do. I just know I can't do that no more."

"Maggie, you never used to be like that."

"I thought you was all about acceptance."

Joey Ratliff geared down to take a hill. "They done something to you in that program. You used to be cool."

"And being cool got me a lot of jail time."

"I can make us some money. I'll pay you."

"I don't need your money. I don't need nothing from you."

"You're gonna need something sometime, because . . ." He paused.

"Because what?"

"I probably shouldn't be telling you this. . . ."

"But you're gonna tell me anyway."

"It's probably none of my business, but . . ."

"You're right, it's none of your business."

"What I'm trying to say . . ."

"If it's some kind of bullshit, I don't want to hear it."

"How long has Gary been out, Maggie?"

"What difference does it make?"

Joey Ratliff shrugged. "I'm just trying to tell you something."

"You're trying to stir up some bullshit is what you're doing."

"I'm just trying to say . . ."

He did not finish what he was trying to say. They reached the top of the hill at a point where the road curved away to the left. Again, the truck swung right and the trailer with it, and again the boy had to wrench the truck off the shoulder. Again, the trailer swung off the gravel of the shoulder and across both lanes.

"Damn," Maggie said. "You're gonna kill us all for sure." The cattle bawled the louder. "These poor cows are getting beat to death."

"They'll be all right."

"They sure don't think so."

"Those old whores'll be hamburger before the week is out."

Maggie looked back at the trailer, then to the boy. "Joey," she said. "I know you don't have no cattle of your own."

Maggie heard just the slightest hesitation in his voice. "Dad told me, take these girls to Hillsboro."

"You don't lie good, do you?"

"What're you saying, Maggie?"

"You don't lie good. If you're gonna lie, do it right."

"Who says I'm lying?"

"It ain't hard to tell. You're stealing your daddy's cattle."

"Maggie, that ain't true."

"You owe some money to the boys in town."

"Naw, Maggie."

"Them boys is out to hurt you, so you're gonna sell your daddy's milk cows."

"Maggie . . ."

"But you still want your Oxy, so you want me to hook you up with the boys on the hill cause you ain't burnt them yet."

"Oh fuck, Maggie."

"You're a damn thief."

"Look, Maggie, don't be talking this shit to my dad."

"I got nothing to say to your dad, but I'll say it again to you, you're a fucking liar and a thief."

The boy shot a look at Maggie. "You've got a lot of nerve talking about me after what you did to Gary."

"What are you talking about?"

"Everybody knows he sat up there in jail for six long months so you wouldn't have to go back to prison."

"Joey, shut up."

"Everybody knows he took the rap for you and now he's got a record and he's lost his job and it's all on account of you."

"Shut up, Joey."

"And while he's setting in jail, you're still doing what you do till you get a whole new charge."

"Cause some bitch lied on me."

"And Judge Miller thinks he can save your ass, so he gives you treatment instead of prison."

Maggie clenched her jaw and looked straight ahead.

"So you can talk like you got yourself together. You can talk all you want. But I know you're still the same Maggie Boylan."

"You can stop now, Joey."

He would not. "So don't you be talking about me," he said.

Maggie pressed her hands to her ears, but he would not stop.

"Don't be surprised," he said. "Once you get home. You won't find what you think you're gonna find."

He looked her way to emphasize the point. But it was the wrong moment to take his eyes off the road. A rise, a dip, a curve, one after the other and the trailer lashed back and forth across the lanes.

"Oh, my God," Maggie called.

The truck's right front tire tipped over the shoulder and the shoulder was too deep. The steering wheel ripped through the boy's hands to the right and the truck tilted down into the ditch and mashed to a stop in the buttery mud.

Maggie's seat belt held, but she felt like she had been punched. The cattle bellowed like a grade school band. Maggie glared at the boy but did not yet have the breath to speak.

"Oh, Jesus," the boy said. "I'm screwed."

"I reckon so," Maggie said. Her heart was pounding through her temples.

"How are we gonna get out of this?"

"Ain't no *we* to it, Joey. I'm gone."

"Wait a minute, you gotta help me get out of this ditch."

"I didn't put you in this ditch, I ain't gonna get you out."

There was no one out on the road just now, but it would not be long. Someone was sure to come by and call 911 and here would come the Highway Patrol. Maggie unclipped her seat belt, pulled her backpack from the floor, opened her door, and stepped out.

The ditch was half full of runoff and she soaked her feet and the cuffs of her jeans.

"Good luck, Joey," she said. "I got to go."

"You can't leave me like this."

"Just you watch me," she said. "There's nothing I can do to help you and I'm screwed if I stay."

"Maggie, you're a bitch."

"Accept it, motherfucker." She slammed the truck door and climbed out of the ditch.

"I'm gonna call the judge and let him know you was with me."

"Joey, you're gonna do what you're gonna do and I'm gonna do what I'm gonna do." She stepped to the back of the trailer and peered through the slats.

There must have been half a dozen milk cows crowded one on another. The largest of them raised her head and bawled out a long loud lament.

Maggie drew back the slide bolt that held the tailgate closed, opened the gate, pulled out the ramp, and stood back. Not a one of the cows moved. A coffee-eyed calf lowered her head at Maggie and stared.

"Well, cows," she said. "You're on your own from here." She started up the road toward home. At a hundred yards down the road, she looked back. The coffee-eyed calf stood on the shoulder grazing. Joey Ratliff was still in his seat in the cab with his head against the steering wheel. He was either cursing or praying. Maggie could not tell which.

❖ ❖ ❖

THE HOUSE was cold, but not empty. Gary had taken only what he needed and left the rest to her. He also left a note on the kitchen table.

> *Sorry, Maggie, but enough is enough.*
> *I done all I could and I can't do no more.*
> *I'll be back some time for the table saw,*
> *But I won't stay*
> *Good luck to you,*
> *Gary*

She couldn't blame him. If she had wanted to, she couldn't blame him. They had taken blame away from her in treatment. They had taken her blaming, her lies, her drugs, her thieving, and even, for now, her curses. Her curses on the courthouse lawn were her last.

She was as close now to nothing as she had ever been.

She was wet and chilled through and her pinched feet were sore. She found some dry shoes and socks. Gary had left her some firewood and she fired up the kitchen stove and the wood stove in the parlor. She fixed herself a plate of food but she could not eat. A familiar, queasy, low-feverish feeling had gripped her at bowel and bone.

She could not get rid of the chill, no matter how high she stoked the stove. No matter what she did, she could not rid herself of the daunchy feeling in her gut.

Damn, she thought, I come all this way through the program and I'm dope sick all over again.

It did not help that, every hour, cars came back and forth and up and down to the boys on the hill across the road. Somebody was buying and the boys on the hill were selling. All she had to do to get well was cross the road and climb the hill. She wouldn't even need a dime. They would front her, surely, if only so that she would come back later and pay.

The thought brought her relief and terror all in one.

Call somebody, she remembered. But she had no phone. *Go to a meeting*, she remembered. But she had no car. She was stuck in this little farmhouse where every hour, all through the afternoon and into the night, cars from all across the county rumbled over the creek bridge and rattled the gravel of the lane up to Pillhead Hill.

The hours ached by. She tried to read her Big Book, but the sickness fuddled her cross-eyed and she could make no sense of the words. She forced herself up off the couch and fretted around the kitchen with her broom and a rag until there was nothing left to clean. She stood and pondered, What do I do now? How am I gonna get through the night?

From somewhere in the woods or fields nearby, a coyote set up to howl. It sent up a long, lunar lament, made up of sirens and saw blades trailed by a ragged string of yodels and yips. It drew all the dogs up and down the holler out to the ends of their chains to answer back with barks and growls.

But the coyote had said what he had to say. He did not bother to respond. Gradually, the dogs, tired of their argument, crawled one by one back under their porches, and were silent.

That's me all over, Maggie thought. My life's been one long howl. And one big ruckus after another.

Her mind was all atumble. She could not not-think, but to think brought up more thoughts than she wanted to live with.

So fuck it, she thought. Fuck it all.

It would be just a short walk down her lane and across the road, over the bridge, and up that Pillhead Hill to the house. The lights would be on and the boys would be happy to see her. And of course, they would front her—one or two, or even three or four—enough to get her through this godawful night.

Without willing it or willing against it, she threw the little jacket across her shoulders and stepped into the yard. Without willing it or willing against it, she crossed the yard. At the edge of the road she stopped, out of old habit, and looked to the right and to the left.

Then, when she looked forward again, she saw the coyote in the road. He had not been there when she looked to the right; he had not been there when she looked to the left. But now, as she looked to cross the road, the coyote stood directly in her path. He must have come up from the bed of the creek, she thought. As if in response to the notion, the coyote shook out his coat and cast a silver spray into the moonlight. Maggie stood frozen in place.

The coyote gazed at her, one forepaw raised, as if he were reading her through and through.

Oh my God, she thought, what the fuck am I doing?

She put her hands to her temples and turned back to the house. She stumbled to the couch and collapsed. Shivering, nauseous, utterly emptied of thought, bereft of either hope or despair, she curled up into herself like a child. "Oh my God," she whispered.

As if it were a prayer.

Pillhead Hill

RONNIE WILSON woke in the dark, at the bottom of a gully, cold and soaked with dew. It was just at the rise of an early summer moon, with the moon near full, and all around to one side of him loomed great, isolated trees and great, round elephantine bales of hay. A black tobacco barn towered at the top of the other, steeper slope. But whose barn? Whose fields were these? He had no idea where he was or what he had done to get there.

I bought me a load of trouble this time, he thought. And by the ache in his head and the stale, unsettled feeling in his gut, he could just about tell what had got him to this place. He pondered a moment what lie he might tell Sheila.

He had lied his way through tough situations before, and he could spin a good lie when he had to. Sometimes he lied just to stay in practice. But he needed a place to start, a little kernel of truth to build on, and it would help if he knew what truths he had to keep and which to avoid. He pulled himself up to sit and he rubbed the ache in his head and he tried to remember. Gradually, it came on him that somewhere nearby, probably just beyond the barn at the top of the hill, there was an old, two-story farmhouse. Some folks from the city, new to this county, had holed up there and they had some good dope and he had partied there with those new folks and their good dope and Sheila had not been happy about it. She was stoned herself on Oxys, as usual, but she had not been happy because the boys from the city had started him to seriously consider how he might quit his factory job and help them sell their good dope. And she was angry that a girl among the new people had flirted with him and angry that he had flirted back, and that girl barely eighteen, if she was that.

They argued, it got ugly, and he stormed out of the house with the nub of a fifth of whiskey in his fist, determined to drink the argument off his mind.

He stopped behind the barn at the top of the slope to suck down the last of the liquor and to take a leak. The whiskey had lit him up good and he waited for it to take him past drunk, past high, past buzzed, and right up into ecstasy. But first, to piss!

How he managed to lose his balance while pissing over the hillside was something he decided he did not want to know. But he did lose his balance, and so he tumbled Jack-and-Jill fashion down the slope and into the gully where he now lay among the reeds and thistles.

So, I reckon all of this ain't dew, he thought.

He sat for a time among the thistles and listened to the trickle of water that ran down to the creek until a new, troubling memory came to him from the time he lay stupefied at the bottom of the hill. It was a vague cloud of a memory crowded with voices, angry voices that grew in their anger. Someone shouted; someone pleaded. Then a rumble of a sound like thunder that went on and on. And then stopped.

❖ ❖ ❖

THE DISTANT sound of guns routed Maggie Boylan from her sleep. For a moment—that groggy moment it took her mind to crawl up from the cave of her dream—she thought the sound was the rip and rumble of thunder. But she knew her weather signs. If this was thunder, it was strange thunder. Moonlight flooded her window. There was not a breath of wind, not a hint of lightning, not a leaf that stirred.

That's not thunder, she thought, that's somebody shooting guns.

Coon hunters up in the hills, she reckoned at first. It was past the season, but it was a clear, crisp night. She held in mind for a moment the image of a man in overalls thrashing through the thickets behind his hounds. But a coon hunter would fire a single shot, maybe a second if the first one failed to bring down the coon. This was a volley of shots. And that first volley was followed by a single shot, then a second, and a third, and more. *Bop. Bop. Bop. Bobop.* Then, silence for a time. Then—*badop*—a quick pair of shots. Then, with a rip like thunder, a final, explosive volley.

God only knows what them boys is up to, she thought.

Them boys were the ones across the road and over the creek and up the long steep lane that led to what they now called Pillhead Hill. She was sober now, almost three months clean and sober, so she did not truck with Pillhead Hill any longer. She had made a decision. Whatever they did on Pillhead Hill was no concern of hers. So she drifted back to sleep.

She woke again when the first siren swooped down from the north like a great, bloody owl and the whoop-a-whoop of it grew and grew until she had to clap her hands over her ears. Then she heard the complaint of tires as the car turned into the lane, then the rumble of the bridge floor and the scratch and rattle of gravel as the first car climbed the hill.

Oh Jesus, she thought. Has some poor fuck gone and overdosed?

In minutes, a second siren wailed up from the south. Others whined, wailed, and whooped in the distance, purling whoop-a-whoop, one on the other, converging from every corner.

She rose and threw on a sweater. She went to the kitchen, lit a cigarette, and stood in the window. She recognized, one after another, the Highway Patrol, the county sheriff, cop cars from various points around, and ambulances from three different volunteer fire departments. Each one wailed down the road, bawled around the turn, rattled the floorboards of the bridge, and scratched its way up the hill. The red and blue lights spilled down the hillside and into the waters of the creek. The mists off the creek were miscolored with them, and the fields, and the trees, the great, round bales of hay in the pasture, and the gravel of her lane. The shambled pickets of her front yard fence were outlined in red and blue light that mixed and spread in a pattern that seemed not of this world. Each of the lights, she knew all too well, had its own pulse. But with so many, and taken all together, the congregated lights had an erratic, stuttering, strained, and unpredictable rhythm like that of a heart in deep distress.

She said a little prayer for the boys who lived on the hill and for whoever had been up there with them.

Oh Jesus, she thought. Please let them be all right.

❖ ❖ ❖

WHEN RONNIE Wilson set out from the house with his nub of whiskey, the moon had been down at the tops of the trees like a watcher peeking over a fence and the light the moon cast was splintered and broken by the branches of the trees. Now, the moon was full-launched into the sky and it spread its unhindered light over the fields. The only dark place was the patch of hillside in the shadow of the barn.

Was it an hour since he tumbled? Two? He guessed, by the position of the moon, that it was no more than that, so he reckoned there was still more party going on. He could hear a distant radio, but nothing of the voices, nothing of the dream-like thunder he had heard before he passed out. The hillside was steep and his path to the house lay in the shadow of the great black barn. And he was still drunk, transcendentally drunk, staggering drunk, so he picked his way slowly and as carefully as drunk would allow, so that he staggered and swayed and stumbled back nearly as far as he moved forward and he wished he had taken just a little hit of speed or a half-line of coke to keep his motor moving.

Then he remembered that half-remembered sound of voices and thunder and he stopped for a while altogether.

❖ ❖ ❖

"WHAT'S THAT, babe? What are you doing?" That was all he
asked when Sheila turned all hatchets and hammers on him.
   "What's it look like I'm doing?"
   "It looks like you just snorted a line. Baby, ain't you done
enough for one night?" He glared toward Randy the Man but
Randy glared back from behind his black brows.
   Randy the Man was the guy from the city who owned this
house with the new people and the connections to bring in the
good dope. He loomed over the kitchen table and flexed his big
wrestler's shoulders, sorting pills with his big, blunt fingers "You
want some?"
   "Naw, man. I'm good." Oxy could get ugly and Ronnie did
not like what Oxy was doing to Sheila. He lifted the fifth of
whiskey he had been sharing with that little, maybe-jailbait girl
in her hippie-chick blouse and ragged-up jeans. A little silver
ring in her navel winked out from under the hem of her blouse
each time she leaned back to take a hit from the fifth and he
was delirious with the sight of it. The girl was a little foreign
in the way she talked and a little babyish in the flesh, enough
that he had to wonder. But she was woman enough in the way
she moved her eyes. Woman enough that Sheila noticed how
Ronnie's eye kept drifting south toward the silver ring in the
girl's navel. She looked at the girl and she looked at him and she
erupted. "Damn," she spat. "This is why you want to quit your
job? So you can trot after this little sorry thing?"
   Sheila went at him buckets and blisters until the OxyContin
kicked in and she suddenly went silent and her eyes went empty.
She waved him away, sat down, and let her hand fall into her lap.
   "So now you ain't even gonna talk to me?"
   She rose from her chair and waved him away again.
"Where's my purse," she said. Her voice had dropped suddenly to
a whisper. "I'm going home." The purse was not hard to find—it
was a big bulky thing covered in spangles. She fumbled in it for
a cigarette, lit the cigarette, slowly inhaled, and said, again, "I'm
going home."
   "No, you're not," he said.

She muttered something else in her voice that had gone
suddenly to a whisper. He could not tell what she said, for she
spoke in an OxyContin mumble. But he could guess, and that
was when he decided he had enough.

"Go if you want or stay if you want," he said. "I'm gonna find
my own damn party."

She stumbled off in one direction and he in another, he with
his bottle in his hand and she with her spangled purse slung over
her shoulder as if she really did mean to go home.

Which she couldn't, since he had the keys to the truck.

But she did whatever she did out the front door of the house
and across the yard toward the road. He did not know what
she did or where she went, for he could not bear to watch her
stumble away with her back turned against him. So he took his
bottle by the neck and shambled off in his own direction.

Randy the Man was still by the kitchen door, still counting
pills into little plastic bags. "She's a grown woman, dude. Don't
look at me."

"I know, I know. I just got to think this shit out, man," he said.

"Do what you gotta do."

Ronnie nodded to Miss Possible Jailbait as he passed her and
he thought she winked at him. It was maybe just a sneak-wink
of a twitch of the eye, nothing more. But yes, once he thought
about it, a definite wink and a sign that, if Sheila really did go
home, he was bound, before the night was over, to get him a
little strange.

❖ ❖ ❖

SO HE was not at all sure what he was staggering toward up this
shadowed hill. Another fight with Sheila? A little knock-around
in the hay with the hope-she's-over-eighteen hippie chick?
Once, he stumbled, and he saw that his empty bottle lay in the
grass. He raised it and saw that it was empty. So he threw it
down the hill and it broke on a rock.

He still heard the radio.

But no other voices.

They must all be wasted, he thought. Catastrophically wasted. There's gonna be some seriously elevated buzzes. This is some serious shit going down.

His own buzz was in serious need of tending. He had lost most of the pleasurable part and he was left with the staggering, stumbling, uncoordinated part and the uncomfortable, headachy, stale-in-the-gut early phases of hangover.

A nice, tight line of coke, another long drink of whiskey, and a little, skinny joint to round it out and take off the rough edges. Then he would see where the rest of the night would go: patch it up with Sheila or let his tongue play with I'm-Sure-She's-Old-Enough's navel ring.

At the top of the hill, he leaned to rest a moment against the barn wall and looked around. Sure enough, there was the farmhouse, just as he remembered. A radio disc jockey prattled away, but there were still no other voices. Lights blazed in all the windows, but he heard no other voices; he saw nothing that moved.

Man, they can't all be totaled, he thought. Cause there's a shitload of dope to be had and the night is young.

There was something like a bale of weed and a crate of liquor and piles of pills of every sort, just waiting to be used and abused.

It's the Grand Central Station of intoxication, he told himself. And I ain't nearly through.

He intended to party straight through the night until morning, to get drunker, higher, more fucked up, wasted, blizzed, ruint, stoned, bombed, tanked, hammered, cranked, looped, and fried than he had ever been. He wanted to get as far away from Ronnie Wilson as he could get and still make it back. He wanted to go straight to the edge.

He had lost valuable time. And he was wasting time now. So he pushed himself up off the side of the barn and staggered toward the farmhouse.

Hell yeah, he told himself. We're gonna party till the last dog dies.

❖   ❖   ❖

DEPUTY SHERIFF Timothy Weatherstone crested Pillhead Hill in his cruiser, siren roaring and light bar blazing. He pulled into the drive that ran between house and barn and saw Ronnie Wilson—from out of nowhere—dead centered in his headlights, his beard and hair all crazylit with red and blue light. Weatherstone hit the brakes hard and came to a stop in a spray of gravel.

Wilson slapped both hands down on the hood of the cruiser and shouted, "Motherfucker, you damn near laid me flat."

But Wilson threw both hands up and backed away when Weatherstone came out with his pistol leveled.

"Holdupholdupholdup," he called.

"Keep your hands where I can see them," Weatherstone shouted back. He looked quick to the left and to the right, just in case, and hoped the crazy in the lights would not notice how his pistol shook. Other sirens railed in the distance, but Weatherstone was the first, and had no idea what he was up against.

Wilson squinted and started to lower his hands. "Timmy," he said, "it's me."

"I said, keep your hands where I can see them."

"Timmy, you dumb motherfucker." He brought his hands back up. "It's Ronnie Wilson."

"Ronnie? And who else?"

Wilson made a crazy sort of half-laugh. "That's just the problem," he said. He seemed to regret his joke right away. "Seriously, man, you got to help me."

Weatherstone lowered the pistol. He had arrested Ronnie Wilson once before and he hadn't been much trouble. But still. "Who else is here?"

"That's just it, man. There's just a mess of shot-up people and I can't find Sheila."

Tim Weatherstone looked toward the farmhouse. The lights were on; a radio played. "Who's in there?"

"A bunch of people with their heads blowed in. Man, you got to help me find Sheila."

The sirens continued to howl down the valley toward them. A second car hit the bridge floor.

"Who are they?"

"I don't even know half of them. Man, it's dead bodies all over the place. And I can't find Sheila nowhere."

"How many wounded?"

"Ain't nobody wounded. Man, they're all dead."

A second car began to scratch its way up the gravel lane. "Hold up," Weatherstone said. He sensed that Wilson was about to run. "Hold up," he said. "Don't go anywhere."

"What if it's the motherfuckers that done all this?

"Then they're coming in a cop car." The car had just switched off its siren; he could hear it moaning to a close. But the lights still slashed the night. "Don't go nowhere," he said again. "This is one of ours."

A State Highway Patrol cruiser crested the hill and cut across the yard and came to a stop with Ronnie Wilson pinned into the intersection of the two sets of headlights. In two seconds, the trooper was out of the car with his pistol raised.

"Keep your hands up where I can see them," the trooper called.

"Man, Timmy, tell him. I'm the one who called 9-1-1."

The trooper nodded to Weatherstone. "I have him covered. Go ahead and cuff him."

"Cuff me?"

Weatherstone hesitated, then pulled the cuffs from the back of his belt.

"Man, I got to find my girlfriend."

"Put your hands behind your back," Weatherstone said.

"Timmy, man, you gotta help me." He looked at Weatherstone as if he had been betrayed. "Timmy, man, you and me been knowing each other since second grade. Man, I just want to know what happened to my girl."

❖ ❖ ❖

THE HIGHWAY patrolman didn't like it, but the sheriff ordered Weatherstone to undo Ronnie's cuffs and sent the two deputies who came with him to search the perimeter for Sheila and whoever else might have survived.

"So tell us what you know."

"I know there's a bunch of people with their heads blowed in and ain't none of them Sheila."

"We'll find her, but we need you to show us where these people are."

"Just walk right in. They're all laid out for you. But I ain't about to go back in there."

The sheriff nodded toward the cuffs still in Weatherstone's hand. Wilson saw the glance and changed his mind.

❖ ❖ ❖

IT WAS a sad, bloody business and Weatherstone, with just six months on the force, had never seen the like and hoped never to see the like again. They counted ten. Two on the porch, two in the parlor, three in the kitchen, a naked couple in an upstairs bedroom, and one more who had tried to hide between two of the cars lined up in a row behind the house.

"Looks like they took everybody by surprise."

"People was so fucked up, they wouldn't of heard a brass band come up that hill," Ronnie said. "I was so fucked up I couldn't stand and that's the only reason I'm still alive."

Each of the victims had taken a well-placed bullet to the head. The naked couple were still in their final, bloody embrace.

"All very neat and proper," said the trooper.

The sheriff asked Wilson. "Can you ID any of these people for me?"

"Ain't none of them Sheila, that's all I know."

But he did know some of them. One was his buddy from work. He had been shot in the back of the head and the bullet tore out half his face on the way out, but Wilson knew him by his big red Irish fro. Randy the Man sat bolt upright at the kitchen table where he had been parsing pills into plastic bags. He had taken a bullet to the middle of the forehead and there was a hint of surprise and irritation in the creases around his eyes; his lip was curled around a curse he never got to speak.

"Last name?" the trooper asked.

"He's just Randy the Man. That's all I know."

"You never asked him his last name?"

"Man, a motherfucker like Randy the Man just tells you what he wants to tell you and you don't ask him nothing else."

Ronnie knew the naked couple, though. "She's got a husband and he's got a wife," he said. "I don't reckon you can keep this part quiet."

"Can't tamper with evidence," the sheriff said.

Weatherstone took down the names and closed his notebook.

"Hold on," Wilson said. "You ain't done."

He led them out to the yard and pointed to the dirt path that led to the barn. "Shine your light over there," he said. The trooper took out his flashlight and beamed it out toward barn. There was a blood-black streak in the dirt track, a scuff line, a sandal cast off.

"Just follow that track up to the barn."

The trooper led his beam up the track another twenty yards to what looked to be a pile of rags just at the door of the barn.

"Go on," Wilson said. "This is as close as I want to get."

It was a girl laid out on her back. Her face was pale as a plaster saint. Her eyes studied the most distant stars. From the look of it, she had probably been running for the barn when they shot her. "My guess," the sheriff said, "they shot her in the legs so she couldn't run. They shot her in the arm so she couldn't crawl." Then, as she begged, or prayed or cursed, they tucked one last shot just under her chin.

The first shots would have laid her helpless. Then she would have had to lie there waiting as they came to finish her off.

"They wanted that one bad," the sheriff said.

❖ ❖ ❖

TIMOTHY WEATHERSTONE had been the first on the scene, but within half an hour, other sirens had bawled up the hill and now the yard between the house and barn was a maze of red and blue and yellow lights. A captain from the State Highway Patrol was here, and two more deputies and a couple ambulances with

EMTs for what good they might do, and even a couple boys from the police department in Union City. The forensic people were on their way down from Columbus and, following procedure, nobody had moved a thing. Ronnie Wilson was locked in the back of Weatherstone's cruiser, damning them all to hell and West Virginia because no one would let him out to go find his girlfriend and Weatherstone's job, for now, was to keep watch on him while the sheriff, the police chief from Union City, and the State Patrol captain stood in a huddle.

"What're they saying?" Ronnie asked.

"Your guess is good as mine."

"They ain't saying, 'Let's go find this boy's girlfriend,' are they?"

"Buddy, I don't know."

The sheriff turned out of the huddle to wave Weatherstone over.

"Tell them," Wilson said. "Tell them Sheila's missing and we got to go find her."

"I'll see what I can do."

"Work him, buddy. Work him."

The sheriff put his hand on his deputy's shoulder. "I want you to go down the hill and fetch Maggie Boylan."

"Why Maggie?"

"If anybody knows who these people are, it's Maggie Boylan," the sheriff said. "It's a wonder she's not up here herself."

"She's not been up there in three months. I see her every day at the Square Deal Grill. If she was getting high, she wouldn't be working."

The sheriff looked dubious. "It's a wonder she wasn't there," he said. "Go fetch her."

❖   ❖   ❖

FETCHING MAGGIE Boylan had never been an easy job. But she was awake and on the porch with a jacket thrown over her shoulders.

"I don't want to go up there," she said.

"Maggie, we need you."

"You just said Ronnie Wilson ID'd most of them."

"Yeah, but Ronnie's drunk as a lord. And he's not all that reliable when he's sober."

"This ain't my problem, Timmy."

"If it was one of yours, wouldn't you want to know?"

"Goddammit, Timmy." She cinched her jacket higher on her shoulders, stepped out onto the porch, and pulled the door to.

"Come on," she said. "Let's get this nightmare started."

In the cruiser, Maggie had to shade her eyes from the glare of red and blue lights. "First time I ever come up this hill riding," she said.

"Always walked it before?"

She nodded. "Or crawled."

"How much clean time you got now?"

"More'n they'll ever get."

They pulled up into the lot and Maggie hesitated, but she got out of the cruiser and looked around at the lights whirling and blending, shadowcasting the men and cars onto the walls of the house and barn.

"This is like the story of my life," she said.

"How's that?"

"One fucking disaster after another."

Weatherstone took Maggie as far as the door of the house. "You sure I gotta do this, Timmy?"

"Come on, Maggie," said the sheriff. "Let's get this thing done."

Maggie glared the sheriff off when he tried to take her by the elbow, so he stepped aside as Maggie stepped into the house on her own.

She came out, twenty minutes later, looking stunned and stunted. A flash of tears crooked down her cheek. Her voice was hoarse. "Can I go home now?"

"Hold on, Maggie," the sheriff said

"I done told you everything I know," she said.

"There's one more." The sheriff pointed toward the barn. He nodded to Weatherstone. "Walk her over there for me," he said. "See if she can ID that girl."

"I reckon that'll be Ronnie's Sheila," Maggie said. She began to mutter too low for Weatherstone to hear, but he could guess.

"It's not Sheila," Weatherstone said.

"That's too bad," said Maggie. "She earned it."

A trooper pulled back the sheet from the pale face of the little rag of a girl and Maggie stopped as if she had been hit with a brick. She grabbed her temples and fell to her knees in the dust.

"Oh God, no," she sobbed out. "Oh Jesus, oh God, oh, what the fuck?"

The trooper wouldn't let her, but she wanted to stroke the dead girl's bloody hair.

"Do you know her, Maggie?"

She did not answer at first. Maggie sat back with her fists balled up and her eyes streaming. "She said they would find her. And she said they would kill her. And sure enough, they did."

❖ ❖ ❖

THE SHERIFF offered her a ride back home with one of the deputies, but Maggie Boylan did not ever want to be in a police car again.

"Suit yourself," the sheriff said. "But don't plan any trips out of town. We might have some more questions."

"I got no answers," Maggie said.

The sheriff raised a skeptical brow.

"If I was to know anything else—which I don't. And if I was to tell you—which I wouldn't—how long do you think it would take before they'd come and thump me in the head like they done this bunch?"

But the sheriff had stopped listening. He had turned toward the shouts and commotion that had risen from the other side of the yard. "Son of a bitch," he said. "There he goes."

For there was Ronnie Wilson zigzagging among the cars in the yard and there was Timmy Weatherstone, a frustrated half-dozen steps behind him.

❖ ❖ ❖

TIM WEATHERSTONE'S inclination was to let Ronnie go
so he could hunt for Sheila, but the State Patrol boys nixed
that. "Investigative detention," they said. They had rank on
everybody else, so they took charge. But all they could get out
of him was a string of curses. "I'll tell you any goddam thing you
want, once you let me find my girlfriend."

"He might be the luckiest druggie in the country, but I think
he knows something he's not telling," said the captain from the
Highway Patrol. So Weatherstone had to lock him in the back
of the cruiser and tell him to wait while they searched, which
none of them, at the moment, was doing.

"Why the hell can't you let me out?"

"Cause the state boys want to question you"

"You can all question my ass," the boy told him.

Weatherstone had no intention of doing anything of the
sort, so he left Ronnie Wilson alone with his curses in the back
of his cruiser.

The forensics had to come all the way from Columbus and
it was the middle of the night. The scene was secured, a long
perimeter of yellow tape was strapped around the whole yard,
including the line of cars. Everyone knew not to tamper with
what was here, so there was nothing to do for now but wait.

He thought, Why not try one more time? He stepped over
to the patrol car and tapped at the window. "If you was to go out
looking for Sheila, where would you start?"

"I'd start from where you'd let me out of this damn car,"

"Look," he told him, "I can't let you out, but I can go myself.
So where do you think she might be?"

He jerked his head in the direction of the road. "Last thing
I know, she said she wanted to go home and she was headed out
the front door."

"So maybe we should call your house."

"Phone's cut off."

"Was she driving?"

"I got the keys."

"So was she gonna walk?"

"I reckon."

"You still on Harper's Run?"

The boy nodded.

"That's five miles at least."

"And she wasn't moving none too fast, neither."

"So she might not be far."

"Let me go and I'll see how far she is."

Weatherstone shook his head.

"So Timmy, how long you plan to keep me in this car?"

"Till somebody tells me I can let you go."

"And when will that be?"

"When they're all done with their questions, I reckon."

"I done already told them I don't know nothing. I didn't do nothing. I didn't see nothing. I didn't hear but that little bit I told them about. When all this was going down, I was passed out at the bottom of the hill."

"And you don't know why somebody might have wanted to kill all those folks."

"Man, it was a party to me and they had a load of dope. That's all I know. John Ambrose from work, he's laying up there with his head blowed in, he says to me, 'Come on out tonight. I know some people gonna party hearty.' So, I gathered up my girl and we went on down. And I never seen so much in the way of drugs. It was the Walmart of mood alteration, man. It was a pharmaceutical fantasy, every dopehead's dream. And I'm thinking, This is the party of my life."

"And you don't know anything more than that."

"You don't think I'd tell you? Timmy, we been knowing each other since we was eight years old."

"What's your point?"

"You could cut me a little slack here."

"And what do you mean by that?"

"I mean, you got me locked in the back of a police car and my girlfriend ain't nowhere to be found and ain't a goddam one of you doing a thing about it so why in hell don't you let me go so I can find her?"

"I'm about to go look myself."

"You couldn't find your ass with both hands."

"Careful."

"What the fuck, I didn't mean it. We can go look together. Just let me the fuck out of here."

"Can't do it."

"Yeah, you can."

"You know I can't."

"Man, you never used to be like this."

"Things change."

Ronnie muttered, "I reckon they do."

"What's that?"

"Nothing, man." He paused. "What about letting me out so I can take a leak?"

"You didn't do too good the last time you went out to take a leak."

"Yeah, I'm a stupid, fallen-down drunk who don't know nothing. But all them smart ones is wearing toe tags."

"You're right. Falling down that hill might have been the smartest thing you ever did."

"So let me out and I promise you I won't fall down no more hills."

"Sorry, buddy."

"Then how bout I piss on your floor?" He crawled up on the seat and made himself ready. "Better yet . . . ," he positioned himself at an angle, "I'll piss through this cage. Which side do you usually sit on?"

"All right, goddammit."

"All right, what?"

"All right I'll let you out. Just hold on a minute."

"Hold on for what? It's coming on me like a freight train."

"Let me get these cuffs on you." He pulled open the patrol car door.

"Now how am I supposed to do the deed with handcuffs on?"

"That's your problem."

"Then how bout I just stay in here and piss up your seats?"

"Come on, then, goddammit."

"All right. All right. All this alcohol, we got the kidneys to working overtime."

Wilson stepped out of the car and started around it, but Weatherstone blocked him with his baton. "That's good right there."

"Do you want to have to walk in it?"

"No, I don't want to walk in it."

"Well, let me step away just a little, at least."

Weatherstone let him pass and Wilson stepped out into the yard a few paces and zipped down his jeans. "You ain't watching, are you?"

"Of course, I'm watching. It's my job."

"Because I didn't think you was that kind of fella."

"You're doing a lot of talking, but I don't hear a lot of pissing."

"Man, I never could piss under pressure. Like all them drug tests."

"Just do it, man."

"Will you just look away for a second? I can't do it with you watching."

Weatherstone sighed and turned his head.

"So I just gotta relax . . . relax . . . relax . . . NOW!"

Wilson shot out across the yard at a run. Startled, Weatherstone hesitated a moment before he swung his baton. He tried a sweep to catch Wilson's feet, but he had leaped ahead of him.

Weatherstone shouted, "He's getting away!" But none of the others was close enough to help. He tried to keep up, but Wilson, powered by drugs and obstinacy, faked him through the maze of red and blue lights, past the yellow crime scene tape and the body of the girl under the sheet, past the squad cars of the Highway Patrol and the town police, past the barn, and straight toward the edge of the hill. Weatherstone fell behind a little more with each fake, but he hoped to catch up in the straightaway.

But too late. With a final leap, Wilson dropped over the edge and out of sight.

Weatherstone ran to the edge of the hill and stopped. Which way did that stupid motherfucker go? He pulled a flashlight from his belt and probed among the willows along the run. Nothing, not a one of them moved.

I've got to find him or my ass is grass, he thought.

And sure enough, half an hour later, after he had twisted an ankle thrashing through the run and soaked himself, the sheriff called him aside.

"How in the world did you let that boy get away?"

"He talked me clean out of my senses."

"He'll do that. But the State Patrol boys is pissed."

"I reckon."

"The captain as much as said you let him go on purpose."

"Well, just let him think that."

"Son, you don't understand. The captain thinking you let him go on purpose is not the same as anybody else thinking it. If he wants to make a case out of it, you've got as much trouble as the boy. He says it don't look good, as he's a friend of yours and he gets away."

"He's not a friend of mine. I went to high school with him is all."

"From the State Patrol point of view, either way, you're cooked. If you let him go on purpose, you're complicit. If you let him go by accident, you're incompetent."

"I don't understand why we're holding him anyway."

"He's the only witness we got."

"He's a witness who didn't see a thing. Didn't hear a thing. Doesn't know a thing. A witness who admits he was stoned out of his mind. What kind of a witness is that?"

"The only one we got. And whoever lost him better find him."

"I slogged through that creek an hour already."

"Best be ready to slog some more. Because you have two hours to bring me back that boy or your badge."

❖ ❖ ❖

I SHOULD of took the ride, Maggie thought.

The moon was still high, but the lane quickly dipped into shadow. Her eyes had gotten used to the multiple lights of the ambulances and the squad cars, so for the first few yards, she found herself folded into a darkness alive with threat. An owl whooped in the distance. A dog barked in a yard down the road. A whip-poor-will alarmed her from the branches of a nearby tree. Some small animal thrashed through the grass.

Each sound, each motion chilled her like a cold hand. She was not about to go back, so she step-stumbled down the lane until her eyes adjusted and the lane came out of shadow.

She had come to the bottom of the hill and was almost to the foot of the bridge when a silvery glint of spangles and a sigh caught her eye and her ear and she froze in her footsteps. The glint and the sigh had come from a patch of tall Johnson grass just a few feet off the lane. Maggie did not want to look, but she stepped closer and she looked. There lay a woman, her purse spangled in the moonlight, lying in the grass, curled up like a baby gone to sleep.

Somebody else they killed, she thought.

In spite of her fear, Maggie stepped closer, parted the Johnson grass, and saw the purse and saw the face.

Oh Jesus, oh fuck, she thought. It's that lying little bitch, Sheila Hacker.

Immediately, she felt a stab of guilt. For Maggie had cursed Sheila Hacker so thoroughly and with such regularity that she was afraid now her curses alone had killed her.

But she must be alive; she moved, she sighed a long, glacial sigh and she had stretched herself out in the Johnson grass.

So, was she wounded? Maggie looked her over. There was no sign of blood. She was alive, barely breathing, her cheek cold to the touch; she was pale in the face, and her lips were turning blue. She had, by the feel of her wrist, only a whisper of a pulse.

I could leave her, Maggie thought. She'd have left me for sure. She would have looked at me and kept on walking. Which is what Maggie made herself ready to do.

She stood, turned, and told herself, Oh fuck it, somebody has to know.

With as much voice as she could manage, she called "Help. Down here. Help!"

The call may have shocked the girl, for she gave a sudden twitch and a gasp and, it seemed, stopped breathing altogether. Maggie called out, "Help!" once more, then knelt down to check. She listened, she felt for breath, she hoped for breath, but there was nothing.

"Heyyyyellp," she yodeled. "Helllp," she called. Her voice gave out and died off to a whisper.

"Dammit," she gasped. "She's gonna die right here." She tapped the girl on the shoulder. "Breathe," she hissed. "Breathe, you bitch."

Damn if she hasn't got me again, she thought. Now what do I do? "Dammit dammit dammit," she whispered. "Breathe dammit breathe."

Ain't this a bitch, Maggie thought. Jesus, this is fucked. Oh my aching Jesus.

She brushed the girl's hair away from her face, rolled her onto her back, and listened one more time. She leaned her face away in the way she had been trained in prison to feel for the girl's breath along her cheek. But she felt nothing. She tilted her head back to clear her airway, and listened again. Not a feather of a breath.

You sorry bitch, she thought.

Then she took a deep breath, so deep it made her lungs hurt, pressed her mouth against the girl's lying mouth, and breathed.

2

RONNIE WILSON found himself again at the bottom of the gully. He was sure, this time, he had broken something. By the feel of it, in several different places. But he had no time to worry over any of them. Tim Weatherstone stood at the top of the hill with a flashlight and a pistol, so he had to run.

Weatherstone shouted, "Ronnie, hold up! You're in enough trouble already."

Wilson wanted to shout back at him, I'm gone to look for Sheila, since none of you sorry bastards will. But other flashlights appeared in the shadow of the barn, so he roused himself and ducked into the thistles.

Nothing, in fact, was broken, but he was sore and disjointed. He still ached in his head and felt queasy in the gut and now he had added new scrapes in his shoulders and knees and all he wanted to do was just lie down. The flashlights had begun to spill down the hillside, so he had to move. But where?

On the opposite hillside, moonlight flared in the spaces in between the bales. It's lit up like Friday night football, he thought. So he had to stay in the brush that collected along the run. He could go upstream—they would not expect that. But he reckoned that the brush would thin out and he would be laid bare. So he had to keep low in the cover of the willows and follow the narrow path of the run. The quickest route, and the one least likely to stir the willows, was straight through the stream itself. He gasped as he stepped into the water. It was colder than he thought it would be, cold for June. He was wearing his heavy, steel-toed boots from work. They soaked through in seconds and turned heavy as lead. But he had no time to worry over it. He could hear the cops cursing their way downhill as they searched the brush. And Tim Weatherstone cursed louder than any of them.

He got used to the cold in a couple minutes, but the water got deeper as he got closer to the road, so he had to slog through the bed of the run, half blind because the brush blocked the moonlight, and he stumbled, soaked his sleeves, cursed, and kept on staggering.

A nice line of coke right now, he thought, would really do the job.

❖ ❖ ❖

TIM WEATHERSTONE saw nothing, but he heard the sound of someone sucking air like a runner, and then a string of hoarse curses, and knew, by the hushed intensity of the curses that it had to be Maggie Boylan.

"Maggie," he called. "What is it?"

"Oh, God," she croaked. "Do you motherfuckers ever listen to anything but the swinging of your dicks?"

"What's going on?"

"I found your missing girl, but the bitch won't breathe."

He parted the Johnson grass and there was Maggie on her knees beside the missing girl.

He got on his radio and called up the hill.

Maggie leaned back into her task; the breast of the girl rose and fell once more.

"I can't get her to breathe," she said. "I can't get this bitch to breathe."

❖ ❖ ❖

IT COULD have been me, Maggie thought. Maybe it should have been me.

The medics rolled out a gurney, lifted the girl, and strapped her to it. Then they loaded her into the ambulance. Maggie stepped aside to let the ambulance pass. The siren began to roar and blood-colored light flared across the fields. The ambulance rattled the boards of the bridge floor, picked up speed, and slung red light down the valley toward the main road. She followed, crossed the bridge and stood in the road to watch the ambulance and to listen to the waning siren.

The moon had risen yet higher. It was getting late. Edie O'Leary would be picking her up for work in just a few hours. She wouldn't take any excuses, either. So Maggie had to get some sleep. But there was no point in trying to sleep when the night was discolored with whirling red and blue light and the air was perturbed with sirens. She watched until the ambulance was just a trickle of light against the black hills. As she watched, a man emerged from the shadowed willows below the bridge. He looked her way a moment, and she was afraid. But he looked away from her toward the disappearing ambulance, then dropped into the willows of the other side.

❖ ❖ ❖

MAGGIE BOYLAN had just descended into dream when she heard the knock at her door. In her dream, the girl beneath the bloody sheet walked again with her wounds all agape. There was a tongue in each wound and each wound was a mouth, and all the mouths were talking at once in the girl's confounding clabberjabber of foreign.

What are you saying? DreamMaggie asked the dream girl, What are you trying to tell me? The girl tried to talk; she gaped and struggled. But the killers had cut the chords of her throat and no words came to her mouth. There were only the speaking wounds that knew no English.

What is it? Maggie wanted to know, What the fuck are you trying to tell me?

The dream girl tried. She opened her mouth to speak and it almost seemed that she might be able to speak, that she might be able to carry her voice over the clamoring wounds.

But then came the knock at her front door.

The dream girl gasped. Her eyes went wide and she backed away and faded and Maggie was left in that interdream state where the half-sleeping dreamer tries to make sense of what intrudes into the dream, even as the dream retreats and fades.

Again, the knock, a rattlish, metallic, dream-piercing screen-door knock. Not a polite knuckle knock, but a blade of the fist, pound-like-a-hammer knock. And a voice, calling at a level just above a whisper, "Maggie, Maggie, let me in." The dream girl and her wounds were gone and Maggie was awake and full frozen into her bed for fear.

More trouble, she thought.

Carefully, so as to give no sign of her movement, Maggie pulled a robe around her and stepped to the front room. The form in her window was the form of Ronnie Wilson and the voice that whispered, "Maggie, Maggie," was the voice of Ronnie Wilson.

How much trouble, she thought, can one night hold?

She tiptoed to the corner where her shotgun stood, then paused a moment and listened again.

"Maggie, please, let me in."

Quietly, she broke down the shotgun, took a deer slug off the shelf, and loaded.

"Maggie," he said again in a hoarse, just-above-a-whisper voice, "I'm about to die out here of the cold."

She remained in the shadows where she was sure he could not see her and called out, "Ronnie, I don't know what you're doing on my front porch at this hour of the night, but you'd better move on before I call those cops from off the hill."

"Maggie, you never called a cop in your life."

"Things change."

"Maggie, "I'm trying to find Sheila."

"She's already found."

"Do you know that? Is she all right? Don't play."

"You mean, you don't know?"

"Maggie, you're killing me. Is she all right?"

This sorry son of a bitch, she thought. She cradled her shotgun in one arm and opened the door. "You might as well come in. Everything else has gone wrong."

"Is she okay?" Ronnie's britches were wet and muddy at the knees and his hair was full of twigs and bits of dried leaf.

"You been on a snipe hunt?"

"I been on a girlfriend hunt ever since they killed all those people. Do you know what happened up there on that hill?"

"Yes, I know what happened. They drug me up there to ID the lot of them. What happened to you? You look like they drug you through the ditch."

"They might as well have. The cops run me all the way here and they might be here any minute looking for me."

"Ronnie, if you got something to do with this . . ."

"Maggie, I swear I don't. They'd have killed me too if they'd found me."

"Ronnie, I don't know what you're here for, but I got three years on the shelf. Three years, and the biggest thing that judge told me was no contact with known users or sellers of drugs or alcohol. And buddy, you are known. I can't be seen with the likes of you for two minutes."

"Well then, just tell me is Sheila okay?"

"I don't know, but you got to get out of here."

"But you said they found her."

"They didn't find her. I did. Now, go on."

"So how come you don't know if she's okay?"

"Because I don't know. I just seen them drive her off in an ambulance."

"And was she shot?"

"No, she wasn't shot."

"You're sure?"

"Sure as I'm standing here."

"Well then she was okay."

"I don't know that."

"Well, what the fuck do you know?"

"I know I got to get you out of my house before five-o comes looking for you."

"Fuck you, Maggie Boylan. I try to ask you a simple question about my girlfriend and all you give me is riddles."

"Fuck you back. I never told you riddle one. You just riddled your own damn self. If you'll listen, which I doubt, I'll tell you what I know, which is—are you listening?—she was fixing to turn blue when I found her passed out at the bottom of the hill. She was down in the Johnson grass or they'd have plugged her too. But they didn't, so I mouth-to-mouthed the bitch for an hour—a full fucking hour—or she wouldn't have been alive when the ambulance people come and got her. And after that, whatever happened to the bitch—yes, you heard me say that— whatever happened to the bitch after that is something I don't know and I don't care to know, because I did my duty by her and now the further I stay away from that hussy the better I feel and pardon me for spitting, but I just want the taste of her out of my mouth."

"Damn, Maggie, you've gone total bitch."

"You would know one."

"Fuck you, Maggie. Fuck you entirely."

"And now you can get the fuck out of my house."

"Maggie, I ask you one time as a friend to help me out and you dig up some old shit that didn't mean nothing."

My God, she thought. Was I that ignorant when I was still using? "This ain't no old shit. This is right now. Her lying ass got me three years on probation which'll turn into three years in prison if you don't get off this porch in half a minute."

"Maggie, I didn't have nothing to do with her testifying against you."

"You sure didn't stop her."

"Maggie, I ain't never been able to stop her from nothing. I tried to keep her off the Oxys, but somebody . . . let me think . . . who was it got her started?"

"You prick. Now you can get out of my house for sure."

"Maggie, they're looking for me out there."

"I'm sorry for your little problem."

"Maggie, just help me get to the hospital."

"On what? My magic horse?"

"You got a couple cars back there."

"If either of them would start and I didn't have a suspended license and if I gave a shit about you and your problem, I might drive you up there. But right now, I couldn't ride you to the mailbox."

"Maggie . . ."

"So go on. What do I have to do to make my point?" She raised the shotgun. "I got a deer slug in here that'll cut through your liver like a hot knife through butter. So, get out of here and down the road."

She was afraid she really would shoot him, so she pointed the gun just to his left, but close enough. Ronnie raised his hands. "All right. All right. All right," he said. "You don't have to tell me twice."

He backed out the door and into the night.

❖ ❖ ❖

THE DREAM girl's wounds had not yet begun to speak again when Maggie heard the next knock at the door. It was Tim Weatherstone this time.

Please, God, no more bodies, she thought.

She opened the door just a crack. "What now?"

"We're looking for Ronnie Wilson."

"Ain't seen him," she said. The lie came easy as ever. "I don't want to see him."

"Have you seen anybody lurking around, looking suspicious?"

"I just been trying to sleep. I got to work in the morning. I ain't got time for suspicious people or nothing suspicious."

"Well, I got to find him."

"Can I shoot him if I see him?"

"Naw, I need him first."

"You're welcome to him. I got no use for the sonofabitch."

Weatherstone pitched the beam of his flashlight along the exhausted pickets of her front fence. "He's a slick one. He might be right out here listening to us and we never even know it."

"And do you think he had something to do with all of this?"

"No, he's harmless. But he's as close to a witness as we've got."

"Well, if I see the motherfucker, he's yours."

"Thanks, Maggie. You're a sweetheart."

"Yeah, tell me what you really think. Now, can I go back to sleep?"

"Here, Maggie, take my number. If you see him or hear from him, call me."

Maggie took the card and nodded. She did not tell him that her phone had been cut off. She just nodded and slowly closed the door. She went to the window and watched him follow the beam of his flashlight down the ditches and back and forth and across the road. When he was out of earshot, she gave a low whistle. "Come on out, Ronnie," she said.

There was a stirring from beneath the porch and Ronnie Wilson squeezed out through a gap in the porch facing. He pulled himself to his feet and stood, his jeans and jacket even

more clotted with mud, his hair and beard even more tangled
with leaf and twig.

"How'd you know I was there?"

"Do you ever do what you're told?"

"Is he gone?"

"He's gone for now."

"You reckon he'll come back?"

"I don't know. But I don't think he believed me."

"So what do you think I ought to do?"

"What part of 'get out of here' don't you understand?"

"And what if I don't?"

"I still got this shotgun."

"Maggie, you've done a lot of things in your life, but
shooting an unarmed alcoholic ain't one of them."

"Well, get the hell in here before I shoot you for real."

"What we gonna do, Maggie?"

"Get out of those filthy clothes and take a bath and I'll find
you something Gary left."

❖   ❖   ❖

HIS TWO hours were up. Tim Weatherstone stood at the foot
of Pillhead Hill and looked up to where the blue lights and the
red lights carnivalized the hilltop. His feet had grown heavy,
his head dizzy. The thought of climbing that hill felt something
like a death. He stood for several minutes, deep in thought. The
waters rattled in the creek behind him. An owl hooted in the
woods beyond.

It's over, he thought. I worked for years to get this. And now,
just like that, it's over.

3

THE SHERIFF stood in a small circle with the State Patrol
captain, a couple of the detectives from Portsmouth, and a
man in a rumpled suit. Weatherstone stood a few feet away
and waved the sheriff over. The sheriff looked to the State
Patrol captain and the captain nodded, so the sheriff followed

Weatherstone to the edge of the circle of lights where they could talk without being heard.

"I'll turn this in to you," Weatherstone said. "But not in front of them." He had already taken the badge off his shirt and now he handed it over. The sheriff took it and stuck it in his pocket. "So you never found him?"

Weatherstone unbuckled his gun belt, coiled the belt around the pistol, and handed that over as well. Finally, he took the keys to his cruiser from his pocket and handed those over. "I'll send the uniform over."

"Hold onto it. This is just procedure. It'll all clear up in a day or two."

"You'll have to get somebody to cover my shifts."

"A day, maybe two. This'll all go away."

"I'll write up my report and send it along."

"Yes, do that. I'll need the part about that boy escaping, too."

"It'll be in the report." He nodded toward the circle of men. "Who's the one in the suit?"

The one in the suit was having trouble standing straight, but no one seemed to notice. He shook hands woozily all around, then pulled a set of keys out of his pocket.

"That's Miller, the judge, isn't it?"

The sheriff seemed not to hear the question. "This won't last," he said.

"What's Miller doing here?"

The judge gave a brief, boozy wave to the sheriff and started toward the row of cars lined up behind the house. He stumbled and stalked out of the tent of light to a black SUV at the end of the row. A trooper followed with a flashlight and together they examined fender, door panel, fender, tailgate, fender, door panel, fender, grill. Satisfied, the judge got into the driver's seat and started the engine.

"Can he do that?"

"He's a judge, son. He can do what he wants."

The judge waved briefly to the sheriff, then steered past the circle of men in the wheelhouse lights, and started down the drive. A deputy lifted the yellow band of crime scene tape and he passed under and started down the hill.

"You've had a rough night," the sheriff said.

"Not as rough as some others, I reckon."

"Rough enough. I'll get somebody to take you home."

"That's all right. I'm not that far."

They heard the SUV rattle the bridge floor, scratch up the gravel of the lane, then turn onto the road.

"You didn't see what you just seen," the sheriff said.

"I didn't see a judge drive away with possible evidence from a crime scene?"

"You didn't see what you just seen. Remember that."

Weatherstone said nothing. The judge worked his gears, first, second, third, all the way up the road.

"When did you want that report?"

"Don't worry about it. I got you covered."

❖ ❖ ❖

RONNIE WILSON raised his head to get a peek out the window of the car but Edie O'Leary caught him in her rearview mirror. "Ronnie," she said. "Keep your damn head down."

Maggie Boylan, riding shotgun, turned and glared. "Stay down where they can't see you," she said.

"But there ain't nobody out there to see me." In the quick glimpse he got before Edie ordered him down, Ronnie saw pasture to the one side and the moonlit sabers of new tobacco to the other.

"Ronnie, just do what we tell you," Maggie said.

He sank back into his seat. "I was just trying to see where we were."

"All you had to do was ask."

"I did. You and Edie was too busy arguing to hear me."

"If you keep popping your head up, the jailhouse is where we're all gonna be."

"Well, how much further we got to go?"

"Ronnie, we ain't even come to the highway yet."

"Well, damn," he said. "Pour the coal to it."

Edie O'Leary hit the brakes and the car lurched to a stop and pitched Ronnie off the seat and into the dust of the floorboard.

"Look," Maggie said. "You duck-brained sonofabitch. If you don't like the way she's driving, you can get out right here and hitch you a ride with the Highway Patrol."

Ronnie pried himself off the floorboards, crawled back into the seat, and lay on his back with his head well below the window line. From there, he had no more than a splinter of a view—some tree branches, some power lines, a patch of cloud illuminated by the moon—and he felt as if he had been stuffed into a box, or as if he had been laid out in an open grave just before they threw down the dirt. His buzz had long ago started to unravel and he was into the jumpy, seasick-on-dry-land, achy, head-bust, all-annoying middle stages of hangover. He dreaded what was yet to come.

Meanwhile, Edie and Maggie argued back and forth. "Kindly and tolerant, my ass," said Maggie. From there, it was Big Book this and resentment that all the way down the road.

"I hope you all know my girlfriend could be dying while you're up there talking all that AA shit. She could already be dead."

But if they heard him, they never let on. Frustrated, he lay back and watched the trees and the power lines and the moonlit clouds roll by.

In a minute or two, Edie and Maggie had argued each other into silence and each of them crowded herself against the car door, as far as they could get from each other and still be in the same car.

Ronnie could stand silence just so long so he said, "Hey Maggie, you know what's weird?"

"Besides what's in the backseat of this car?"

"He could have had me, Maggie."

"What the fuck are you talking about?"

"Tim Weatherstone. All he had to do was reach out and touch me. I was in that little run just about down to where it meets the creek and my one leg sunk down in a mud hole so deep I thought I would keep on going to the other side of the earth. I finally hit rock bottom, but there I was stuck like a duck, trying to pull my leg out and that mud was trying to suck the boot right off my foot and then I caught the light from his badge and I just shrunk down and waited. I know he had to see me and I'm thinking all he's gotta do is stick out the cuffs and I'm done. But he didn't. It was like he just looked me over and went on because when I looked up he wasn't there no more."

"Ronnie, what kind of bullshit are you trying to sell us?"

Something about what Maggie said set Edie off. "There you go again," she said, which set Maggie off, and then they were at it for the rest of the drive.

Finally, he saw the corner of a billboard and knew they were close. He raised his head ever so slightly and saw, to one side, the golf course, and to the other the cemetery. He slid back down into the seat and let the women argue all the way into the parking lot of the hospital.

❖ ❖ ❖

AT AROUND one a.m., James Carpenter finished his rounds and started a letter to his daughter. He doubted he would get a reply—he had gotten no reply to the last three letters—but he thought he might as well try again. If nothing else, it might get some things off his chest. And it would fill the time. He worked the hospital security a few shifts a week, usually the weekends, and almost always second shift or third, and counted himself lucky to get that. Since he was fired as a deputy and had lost all his appeals, there wasn't a department for five counties around that would hire him for deputy or dogcatcher.

Hospital security paid the bills, but it was nothing at all like being a deputy. There wasn't the pay and there weren't the benefits and the uniform didn't fit and he struggled, especially when he worked third shift, with the long, boring, flatline hours. But it was a paycheck and in the quiet hours he could read or think.

He dawdled like a schoolboy with a page of paper in front of him and an ink pen in his hand. The police scanner on the corner of the desk lisped out a steady stream of static. By 1:23, he had gotten only as far as the date at the head of the page. By 1:35, he had scratched onto the page, "Dear Emily, I hope this letter finds you well." And at that, he stalled again.

He raised his ear to the scanner. There had been nothing since eleven p.m. when he started his shift and he expected nothing now, but he liked to listen when he could. He liked to know what was coming—gunshot wound, knife wound, car wreck, saw cut from a lumber mill, saw cut from a chain saw, concussion, contusion, nervous breakdown, a kid who fell out of a tree, a farmer overturned by his tractor, a hunter's foot mangled by a trap. There might be broken noses, broken ankles, bruised wives, fractured skulls; there might be a hand pierced by an arrow, spitted by a catfish fin, sliced by a tobacco knife, bit by a dog, riddled by a shotgun blast; legs amputated by box car, legs broken by a leap from a jailhouse window, knees blown out and a football scholarship gone up in smoke. There might be overdose by OxyContin, Percocet, moonshine, Valium, tequila, Xanax, heroin, Wild Turkey, or a combination of any two or more. Frostbite; heart attack; stroke; seizure; snakebite; poisonings accidental or suspicious; burns of first, second, or third degree; electrocutions by faulty wiring or stroke of lightning; nerves derailed by methamphetamine.

Every sort of human ruin, lifetime or just a bad night, every sort of human pain, accidental or inflicted.

If he hadn't seen it yet, he reckoned it was coming.

❖ ❖ ❖

AT 1:38, Carpenter scratched onto his letter, "I know we've had our differences, but I want you to know . . . " He paused there to consider how to tell her what he wanted her to know, but at 1:39, the scanner began to crackle with word of a multiple shooting out in the county. He dropped his pen and listened hard as the flat, mechanical voice of the dispatcher called on

the sheriff and the sheriff called on the Highway Patrol, out to
a farmhouse on Russel Gap Road, a house he knew well. There
were six, eight, maybe even ten down. This was major. By 1:50,
he heard the first of the outbound sirens and the bugles in his
blood went with them.

He expected to hear the ambulances rolling back shortly
with a load of shot-up people. But by 2:45, none of the
ambulances that had bawled out of town had come back. He
knew what that meant, so he told triage they could relax. No
one was coming.

He made his rounds again. And again, all was quiet in the
Morris County Hospital. The newborns were stretching out their
small lungs and wailing, the sick were healing, the wounded
were mending, and the dying were dying quietly. He looked
back at his unfinished letter. He was convinced now that no
matter what he wrote to his daughter, he would write it wrong.
He balled up the paper and banked a three-pointer into the
wastebasket across the room.

Then, at approximately 3:15, he heard the distant squall
of a siren. The voice on the scanner told him it was an
overdose—the third in a week—and not one of the shootings.
By 3:45, the ambulance rolled up to the door of the ER. The
EMTs jumped out, rolled out a gurney, plunged the gurney
through the ER door, and shot it straight back to intensive
care.

Carpenter caught a glimpse of the girl on the gurney as she
rolled past. Her face was pale as paper and her lips were blue, but
he knew her by the tattoos on her arms and on her hands, by the
ring in her brow, by the face he had known since she was a child;
he knew her step-dad, a drug-running biker turned preacher; he
knew her mother, a feisty, flint-chip of a woman. He knew her
stoner boyfriend.

She's hanging by a thread, he thought, and not likely to
make it. By 4:58, her parents arrived. They conferred briefly
with the triage nurse, and took seats in a corner of the waiting
room where they sat, grave as a pair of headstones.

Carpenter stepped out the ER door and looked around the parking lot and listened. No more sirens. Nothing, no one. He listened for several minutes as the night hawks swept around the arc lamps of the parking lot. He did not know what to make of it all.

At around 5:20, a car pulled into the parking lot. It had barely pulled to a stop before Ronnie Wilson, the stoner boyfriend himself, tumbled out of the backseat and scrambled for the ER door. Close behind came Edie O'Leary and, just after, a muttering Maggie Boylan, glum as dirt, the glare in her eye hard as diamond.

4

IT TOOK Timothy Weatherstone two full days to write his report to the sheriff, for his insomniac pen was slow and it darkened with each page. He wrote, then tore up, and wrote again in the language of reports such as he had learned it in training, that he had received a call while on patrol at 0127 hours and that he had responded affirmatively to the call and, because of the urgent nature of the call, proceeded to the site without waiting for backup and found, held for investigative detention, then, at approximately 0205 hours lost, one Ronnie Wilson, white male, approximately twenty-four years of age and that, at approximately 0247 hours, while searching for said individual, found instead Maggie Boylan, white female, approximately thirty-five years of age, attempting to blow life back into the depressed lung of one Sheila Hacker, white female, approximately twenty-two years of age.

He wrote that he had forgotten, as directed by his immediate supervisor, that he had witnessed, at approximately 0417 hours, in front of several others who presumably had also forgotten that they had witnessed, an individual, white male, approximately forty-five years of age, who approached the sheriff and the ranking Highway Patrol officer on the scene and engaged said officers in conversation and that subsequently said individual, believed to be a judge in the Morris County Courts, drove a family-size, SUV-type vehicle away from the crime scene, in direct violation of state and local law and standard police procedure.

He wrote that he had forgotten, as directed, that he had seen the rich man drive away undisturbed while the poor man was hunted like an animal.

He wrote that he had subsequently come within easy reach of the hunted man but had chosen to let him go, out of an instinct that he did not then understand.

Weatherstone wrote his report, then tore it up and wrote it all again. He wrote for no one in particular, for he never turned it in and the sheriff never asked. He wrote everything he remembered, everything he had done and seen that night. He even wrote that he had walked home, stripped himself of his uniform, flung the pieces of it into the trees and bushes, then stood on his mother's porch, naked as Job, and cursed the sheriff, Ronnie Wilson, life itself, and the day he was born.

He wrote that, just before dawn, he put on civilian clothes and drove his civilian car to the hospital where he found in the ER waiting room, speechless and bereft, the missing individual Ronnie Wilson, along with several other individuals whom he assumed to be friends and relatives of the aforementioned, now deceased, Sheila Hacker. Collapsed into a chair in a corner the aforementioned Maggie Boylan sat, addled with guilt and grief.

He wrote that all those in the room were raging in grief or stupefied in grief and no one seemed to know what to do next until a woman stood and growled them into silence. She had a braid of long gray hair, a face like a chisel, and a voice with the sound of a gravel truck unloading. "Listen up," she shouted, then called everyone to stand, come closer, face each other, and take hands in a circle. For a moment, no one moved.

The woman cut a glance at the man who had been seated next to her. He rose, slow as a boulder, and limped to her side. After him came Edie O'Leary and the security guard from behind his desk and all the maybe-cousins and friends. "Maggie," she called when Maggie Boylan held back. "Come on up, Maggie. You're in this too." Maggie paused, then shuddered off her resistance and stood with the others and they all joined hands in the center of the waiting room.

The woman then prayed a long, rambling, meander of a prayer full of starts and pauses. She sometimes ran with the words and sometimes stumbled; she lost her words and found them and rolled them over in the gravel of her voice. Tim Weatherstone caught them as best he could and wrote them into his report.

He wrote that she told the people in the circle that she had lost her daughter long before she lost her tonight and that she blamed no one and she forgave all as she hoped she would be herself forgiven.

Do not argue, she said. Do not blame. All we have is one another and this is not a time to argue or to blame.

Nothing in this world will last, she said. Nothing in this world will ever be right.

At this, the woman could say no more. And for a long time after, they all stood together in silence and each held tight onto the hand of another.